Keki N. Daruwalla is one of India's foremost poets and writers. His ten volumes of poetry include *Under Orion*, *The Keeper of the Dead* (winner of the Sahitya Akademi Award, 1984), *Landscapes* (winner of the Commonwealth Poetry Award, Asia, 1987) and *The Map-maker*. Among his acclaimed short story collections are *Sword and Abyss* (1979), *The Minister for Permanent Unrest & Other Stories* (1996), and *Love Across the Salt Desert* (2011). His first novel, *For Pepper and Christ*, was shortlisted for the Commonwealth Fiction Prize in 2010.

Daruwalla was awarded the Padma Shri in 2014. Most recently, he was honoured with the Poet Laureate award at the Tata Literature Live! Mumbai Litfest, 2017. His work has been translated into Spanish, Swedish, Magyar, German and Russian.

Going

Stories of Kinship

Keki N. Daruwalla

SPEAKING
TIGER

TIGERBACKS | Speaking Tiger Short Fiction

SPEAKING TIGER BOOKS LLP
125A, Ground Floor, Shahpur Jat, near Asiad Village,
New Delhi 110049

Published by Speaking Tiger in 2022

ISBN: 978-93-5447-295-4
eISBN: 978-93-5447-300-5

10 9 8 7 6 5 4 3 2 1

Typeset in Garamond Premier Pro by SÜRYA, New Delhi
Printed at Chaman Enterprises, New Delhi

I believe that one can never leave home. I believe that one carries the shadows, the dreams, the fears and the dragons of home under one's skin...

—Maya Angelou, *Letter to My Daughter*

Contents

The Brahmaputra Trilogy

I. The White Terror

It was a cold morning and the jetty was veiled with the mist rising from the river. Though it was winter the Brahmaputra was still massive, flecked with foam along the banks. The two men at the jetty were obviously new to the place for they gazed in awe at the mighty river. They were waiting for the steamboat ferry. In 1946 steamboats were still in fashion. The British Collector and the ever-so-British Superintendent of Police (his face was blood-red and so he was considered by the natives as more of a sahib than the Collector) called it the tug. So did sahibs over in the hills at the Tea Planters Club. Their Overseers travelled on the tug. Natives were forbidden from using the term, but that, as you must have guessed, is a joke. They were not familiar with the sahib log's colloquialisms. For them, these Bengali Babus in an Assamese town, it was the 'Pherry'.

The *pherry* was late. For the phlegmatic would-be passengers, that was no novelty. Engine trouble, wet coal, too many passengers, no passengers—anything could cause delay. And if there were Santhals among the passengers, there was always the problem of tickets and language. They often had no money to pay. If they did have the cash they did not know the right amount to fork out and often argued in their own lingo, which the Ferry Master was unfamiliar with. One Bengali Ferry Master had given vent to his feelings: 'Bhery trawbulsoam, bhery trawbulsoam. These phucking plantasun labour are the bane oph my ass.'

As the tug stopped and the passengers flooded out, the two men waiting at the jetty stepped out of the shadows and followed a strapping lad, whose shirt collar was upturned and his muffler was wrapped around his forehead. His name was Vikram. The others followed as if they didn't know him. There was no conversation and no sign talk. They got into a tonga and one of the men in the shadows trotted out the name Jain Dharmashala. The driver threw away the beedi he was smoking and swished his whip over the horse without touching him and drove off. When they reached the dharmashala, they paid off the tonga driver and got in. Before letting the newcomer enter, the caretaker told him only vegetarians are allowed here. We don't want any meat-eaters. No eggs either. The other two, who had stayed here for the night, assured the caretaker and also handed him a rupee note.

When they were alone, Vikram asked the other two—Barua and Bhowmik—why they had stayed here. Weren't we asked to avoid hotels and dharmashalas? Bhowmik, lean and hollow-cheeked with very intense eyes, answered, 'Where else could we have stayed for the night, on the railway platform? The police were roaming there.'

Barua spoke up. 'You did well covering much

of your face with a muffler. We are worried about your skin—I didn't realize you were so fair, though Bhowmik had told me, but still I was not prepared for this. People will think you are a gora.'

'Aren't you feeling cold? You're just in a shirt.'

'I'll manage,' said Vikram.

'Now there are two of us who have to be careful. I belong to Sibsagar. You never know when you run across some old schoolmate.'

'And you think I am a stranger to Dibrugarh?'

Vikram's tone was sneering. Barua gasped. Barua looked like a middleweight wrestler, stocky with no flab. He was all muscle.

'Have you lived in Dibrugarh?'

Vikram didn't think it worth his while to answer. Barua was trying to size him up, this fellow who looked every inch an Anglo-Indian but talked like some rickshaw-puller or coolie. He could belong to any place, from Calcutta to some nondescript town in Assam—Jorhat or Tezpur or something like that. They ordered some tea and got a steaming pot of milky tea. Vikram took one look at it and made a sour face.

'When will they learn to make good tea in Assam?'

Barua didn't like that, but tried not to show it. He just stared expressionlessly at the teapot. Bhowmik thought he should break in. 'Let us leave Assam out of it.'

'Why?' asked Vikram, pointing towards Barua. 'Because he doesn't like it?' He sneered some more and then broke into Assamese. 'I am more Assamese than him.'

Barua wanted to smile, but didn't. It would have been nice to dig into this little pseudo mystery—the white skin and the down-to-earth plebeian or tea garden accent. But his peers did not encourage curiosity and he didn't like the fellow in any case.

'We must move out to look things over,' said Vikram.

'Are you carrying everything with you?' asked Bhowmik.

'I am carrying everything with me.'

'Me too,' said Barua, who in this particular field was held in considerable respect—he had after all derailed an express train some years ago—1942 to be precise. He was wild those days, wild and undisciplined. He had sobered down now.

'Are you clear about what you want us to do? Whom are we taking on?' asked Barua.

'It's a gora,' said Vikram.

'Real gora, I hope.'

'You think I don't understand what you mean,' Vikram let go with some expletives. Then he cooled down and said, 'Yes it's a real gora. Speaks English.'

'Where are we going?'

'Cuthbert Tea Estate.'

Bhowmik's eyes widened. They produced one of the finest teas in the country. The brand was well known.

They didn't want to take a bus. It took them a good four hours, walking through scrub and pine and tea gardens, avoiding roads, to reach a clump of ragged teashops—mud walls and thatch roofs and a hen with her chicks clucking away. Vikram recognized the place. They had some tea there and then set out for the estate. There was no cover of any kind here, nothing but tea bushes and a straggle of trees along the road. The land undulated and rippled away in gently rounded slopes, which from the air could have been mistaken for downs. Vikram pointed out the manager's house, a big, sprawling, one-storied house that seemed to be a part of the rounded curves of the landscape. It had a tiled roof, and a glazed verandah at the back. The house had a brick wall in front and a bamboo fence in the rear. It had two gates and a curved driveway leading to a concrete porch. Vikram recollected that the porch was not there when he was here last.

'We want him, do we?' asked Barua, pointing to the house. Vikram nodded. 'What is he accused of?'

'Atrocities.' Vikram wasn't being too communicative.

'When was it you were here last?'

'Ten years,' Vikram answered.

'You were here for ten years?'

'No.'

'The last you saw the place was ten years back, right?'

'Right,' Vikram answered.

'Ten years is a lot of time.'

'I know, its 120 months and 3,650 days!'

Barua wanted to kick his ass, but kept himself in check. 'What I am trying to say is things could have changed.'

'How?'

'The man may simply not be there,' Bhowmik now joined in. 'He could have gone—left for England. Or he could have changed.' The fellow was making no sense, thought Vikram. But that is exactly what the two of them thought of this whiter-than-milk Vikram.

'There is always a gora sahib here, I tell you, and they are all the same. We will get the next one. How does it matter?'

Barua now lost his temper. 'Ten years! Means you are ten years out of date! You must be mad to bring us here. Never heard of such nonsense. I am opting out! D'you hear, out!'

Bhowmik intervened. He'd go and make enquiries. They went back to the teashops and had lunch—rice and lentils and some watery chicken curry floating in enamel plates from which the paint was flaking off. Bhowmik was just going off when Barua said that Bhowmik didn't know the language. He'd talk in Bangla—it made no sense. Barua decided to go with him. Vikram couldn't say anything and hung around. He had to hang around for over three hours.

The two of them didn't have an easy time. They stood out, despite the rough cotton sheets in which they were wrapped. They looked neither like labour nor like management. Their queries remained unanswered. The women tea workers, the leaf pickers moved away when they were approached. Their questions were answered by questions. They were asked in turn, 'What exactly do you want to know? Where are you from? Why are you asking?'

'Is the Sahib here a gora?' asked Bhowmik finally, not willing to beat about the tea bush any longer. He was the wrong person to ask.

'Why do you want to know?' the worker shot back in Assamese. 'You want some of your own Bengalis to get in? First we get Santhals, then Biharis. Now you want to get your people in. Bloody pimp.'

It was no use, the two of them said, when they met Vikram. Vikram couldn't believe it. Three hours and more, and they couldn't find out such a small thing.

'It is final,' said Barua, 'we are calling it off. No more of this nonsense.'

'No more of what nonsense?' Vikram was trembling with rage.

'We should be looking for the SP, the Collector. Instead we run after some planter, not knowing who he is. No idea whatsoever—is he chalk, is he cheese, is he pork, is he beef?'

'You just want to run, don't you? Run Barua, *bhag* Barua.'

But it was Vikram who ran. The other two were stunned and just looked at each other's faces. Then they also hared off behind him, for he was making straight for the Cuthbert Tea Estate

It had been a sort of death, a mummy-wrap, this skin of his. If only he could strip this white sheath off he would be like the others. But to be white, and at the same time the son of a lowly munshi or a garden worker; to go to a primary school and sit on jute strips on the grass and still be white, that felt like a disease which was incurable. A friend of his, Ahmad, was told by his parents to stay away from him. '*Yeh haraam ka hai*,' the boy was told. He was not kosher. As he grew older he realized what all this meant. Who could his mother have slept with? It was not the kind of question he could easily ask, certainly not of his father, who had taken more and more to the bottle. When in his cups, which was most of the time, he was given over to free kicks directed both at him and his mother. He never used his hands; he just kicked, in the knees, the belly, ribs—wherever his rubber-soled shoe landed. Fortunately the father didn't possess a boot—couldn't afford one. But even the rubber shoe did pretty well judging by the welts and bruises mother and son received every second day.

Memory was a flame and there was a lot of dry tinder in the void of his heart. There was guilt too, for he loved his mother; she was the only one who cared for him. That feeling he had for her itself became a thing of guilt in time; affection in the suburbs and hate at the core could tie up a mature person in horrible tangles. He was hardly out of his teens. He couldn't at the same time forget her tenderness towards him and others. He remembered her feeding the pigeons in the yard. When the feed was over she would shoo them off, and as they rose the whole yard would be darkened with shadows.

It was dusk now. Twilight bled. Even the tea garden seemed to catch a touch of the flame. Barua and Bhowmik couldn't catch up with him. He was far too robust and athletic for them. They gave up, though they were in sight of the bungalow at the Cuthbert Tea Estate. The two of them were panting hard and they were nervous. Why on earth they were saddled with this erratic fool, they couldn't understand. What was the man up to? Was he mad? Then they heard the bomb.

Not just the bomb, but the tinkle of the rain of splintered glass that followed, the shouting and the screams that followed, and the thud of footsteps either scampering towards the bungalow or fleeing from it. There was noise all around; even smoke that rose from the bungalow seemed to be noisy. People were peering over the front wall of the bungalow. Some were clambering over it. The two looked at each other—that's all they seemed to have done this afternoon—in wonderment. They waited for a while. But Vikram was dashing off the other way. There was no point waiting now. They turned and sauntered off. Running would be dangerous.

The steam from the tug was spiralling up. An Assamese poet had talked of the 'morning ferry berthed on the banks of the dawn'. The planks from the wharf were being removed as four policemen, their .410 muskets at the ready, ran towards it shouting for the Ferry Master to wait. They were fat and sweating. They were also huffing and puffing, a talent bestowed on the heavier amongst humankind. As they clambered onto the ferry, someone elbowed his way to the stern and jumped. It took some time for the constabulary to realize what had happened. It took them some more time to muscle their way through the crowded ferry. It took them some more time to load their muskets. Then they let go. The bullets went plop, plop, plop into the Brahmaputra. Each bullet sent up its little fount of spray. The passengers gawked and instead of giving the policemen enough elbowroom to fire freely, crowded round them and constricted their movements.

The passengers were shouting away, some cheered for the runaway, some for the policemen, as each bullet was fired. This was better than cinema they paid eight annas to watch. The river was making its own noise. What was he like, what was he like? shouted the policemen. After some minutes, when the hubbub had subsided, they asked if anyone had seen the fellow. Was he white? A woman raised her hand. 'He seemed to have come out of a coal-hole.' Black? the policemen asked in dismay. Black, she answered. But he threw away his shawl as he jumped, and his arms were white. Some others came up with similar assertions. Must have painted his face black, the bastard, said one of the cops. But his boss, the Head Constable with two stripes on his arm, was depressed. 'We couldn't get him. It is our faces which are blackened.'

He looked back pensively at the vista, bits of mist clotting over the raging Brahmaputra, its banks smothered in foam, the smoke from the tug curling away and moving upriver with the breeze.

II. Leonidas Campbell

I miss her. To miss her is also to miss her music—and I mean her music, not her voice. I miss watching her long tapering fingers on the piano, sliding along the keys, turning that special music out of wood and ivory. But when she sang or even hummed, she could teeter on the edge of being off-key. Surprising, isn't it—when she played Liszt's *Hungarian Rhapsodies*, she could make the piano sing. (It was she who told me—this was before I left for India—that Franz Liszt played with green silk gloves on, and would leave them on the piano after the performance; and the hoi polloi among the ladies would fight over the gloves. Faces got scratched and eyes gouged over those green silk gloves—that's the spice I added. What's the good of a story without spice?)

Obviously, more than I miss her music, I miss her. She was not beautiful. She was thin and tall with a lightly freckled skin and slightly elongated jaw. Once at a party I overheard a woman remarking rather cattily that she was horse-faced. I never thought so. I miss her—I wish I were not repeating that endlessly. And it can be very lonely in the tea gardens here. A few days before I was to leave for India, I went to her flat in Chelsea.

'What will you *do* in India?' she had asked. (She, of course, knew I was going to manage a tea estate.) It was not the question but the look of incomprehension that flickered over her face which irritated me.

'I am not going among the Goths and the Huns, you know, just Indians; soft, malleable Indians.'

'Putty?'

'Well, not exactly. They can be very emotional—and good at speeches. Deprive an Indian of food—he's been without it for centuries—and he won't say boo. Push him off the stage before he has made his speech and you have an enemy for life. Why are you laughing? They love rhetoric. It's all about Dominion status these days. They won't manage it. You need a culture at your back to get on in the world today.'

'They have a bit of it you know, the Vedas and all that,' she said.

'Yes, yes I know. They also have that Maha something something. But I was not talking of culture in that sense, a hymn to fire and another to the wind-gods—maruts they called them...'

'You've been studying them, have you now?'

'Yes, as I was saying before you interrupted me...now what on earth was I saying?'

'Culture.'

'Yes, I mean democratic culture.'

'Yes, they haven't started from rotten boroughs, have they?'

'You can be irritating sometimes, Patricia. I don't know what your father would say if he heard what you said.'

'I said nothing, Len.'

'Well, if he heard what you left unsaid.' Her father was a Tory MP.

'I don't agree with everything he says or does and I have let him know that—more than once. If I were in politics I would back Labour. Anyway, what are you going to do in India with a name like Leonidas?'

'I'll manage. I suppose I'll be Len to the planters and Leon Sahib to the natives.'

'And what will you be to the civil service, the ICS, I mean?'

'Oh, they can kiss my arse.'

'Have you considered the possibility that they might not want to?'

'They can go to hell. They're the least of my concerns. And what, if I may ask, are you going to do in India with a name like Patricia?'

She looked stunned for a moment, almost horror-stricken. 'Are you proposing, Len? I'll be damned. It's the most mundane, colourless proposal I've heard of. What a slimy, insidious way of sounding me. You're supposed to go down on your knees.'

'I will,' I said, 'but I haven't got a ring.'

'Well then, bring one, damn you!'

After a year at Dibrugarh and getting to know the scene, I went back and got married and brought her. In a bitchy moment my sister had said to me, 'I don't know what you see in her except that she is the daughter of her father.' I didn't waste my time telling her that neither she nor I wanted any part of that Tory MP. But I did tell her that once I had asked Patricia what she saw in me.

'And what did she say?'

'My leonine hair, that's what she said.'

Jane, that's my sister, looked at me with the kind of contempt that would have turned a maple leaf brown in mid summer. I had never asked Pat, but I think it was my record in the War, the mention in dispatches, which had kindled her interest in me. I was never wounded, of course. Had that been the case many others would have, shall we say, got interested in me.

The locals couldn't call her Pat Memsahib, and least of all Patricia Memsahib. So they just made do with 'Leon Memsahib'. The first two years or so she loved the place—blue skies, the greenery, friendly ever-smiling people. She didn't care too much for the folks at the Planters Club but didn't show her disdain, not even to me. But I sensed that she found some of them coarse. Initially there were the seasons to look forward to. She had heard so much about the downpours—the sky coming down with the rains as it were. One summer I took her to Darjeeling and the next we trekked into Sikkim.

Within two years she seemed to tire. Her freckles got a redder tinge to them and thus became a wee bit more prominent, whether due to the sun or malaria, I am not sure. We can take leave and go back for a while, I urged but she wouldn't hear of it. She soldiered on for another two years, or was it three? By then malaria had taken over, so to say. Her walks stopped, fatigue seemed to set in by evening, just the time I returned. She started drinking a little more than little and I told her she was making things hard for herself—malaria was tough on the kidneys. If she had got tired of Assam or Calcutta or India I could have understood and gone back home with her and tried my fortunes there. But I think she wanted to be rid of both malaria and me, and perhaps not in that order.

She went back. Now it was my turn to 'soldier on'—I still took my morning walk, knocked back my 'chhota' in the evening and dressed for dinner. I insisted on my usual cup of coffee after dinner. There was no question about letting the staff—butler, cook, maid and gardener—know that anything had changed: frozen lower lip clamped on stiff upper lip, what?

All the same I missed her every minute. At work I would think of the empty house, and her music, which somehow filled the house and all its empty spaces, just as it filled the spaces in my memory. The queer thing was that when I returned I would find the house even emptier.

The bungalow had so many outhouses that Pat and I hadn't known what to do with them. An empty outhouse can be an invitation to fishy happenings. So it was. Someone had brought in a woman for a one-night stand. The butler reported the matter to me the next day. Better get someone in there, Sahib. In an adjoining estate there was a lowly accountant they called 'Munshi', who kept the labour muster roll. He was in some sort of trouble. The butler had gone up to Pat and told her about him. Pat, of all things, interviewed the wife. She found her pleasant-looking and well-dressed. She had clearly married beneath her station. Without my knowing she gave the outhouse, its walls green with moss, to the Munshi. His name was Ganesh, the wife's Anusuya. I had been confronted with the news when I had returned in the evening and couldn't say much bar that I could have been consulted. I made some casual enquiries and found he hadn't filched any money. And Anusuya, whom Pat called Ann, got on rather well with her, both knitting away in the winter sun, Pat on a cane chair under the sun umbrella and Anusuya on a lowly reed stool.

The one thing that had struck me when I saw her for the first time was the almost glossy face, the skin light brown and smooth as silk. But I had never given her another thought. I was fighting my own battle once Pat left. My boss in Calcutta told me, 'Careful, old boy, this is the time you could fall into odd ways.' He had tried to pass it off as a joke but the stare, which followed the words, showed that he meant what he said. Things were telling on me. I wanted to stop shaving. I wanted to throw that damned necktie off—it had started giving me the feel of a ligature now. I was keeping afloat by saying to myself every morning—I WILL NOT GO TO SEED!

A good two years after Patricia had left, the cook fell ill. He was a Muslim called Hameed. I never asked him to fry sausages. Indians in any case don't know how to fry them. They put butter in the pan! I just put them in a dry frying pan and would prick them with a fork so that they fried in their own fat. As I just said, Hameed fell ill. Anusuya made the tea that evening. It was good tea, just right, and served properly—she had even embroidered a new tea cosy for the pot. Earlier I had heard her chatter with the cook sometimes, and when I had asked him, he said she had wanted to learn how to cook *sahib log's* dishes. When the cook's illness got prolonged, she started cooking regularly, always dressed smartly, with an apron over her sari. She was bold enough to let drop on two occasions that I was too alone and should 'import' (her phrase) another Memsahib from England. (During my worst days I wouldn't even read, but just stare at the twilight from the verandah.) The third time she used the word 'import' I instinctively put my palm on that smooth-as-velvet cheek of hers. She caught my palm, turned her lips towards it and kissed it.

The butler left after dinner that evening, saying she would make my coffee. When she came in she had obviously had a bath because her hair was still not dry. She served me a good cup of coffee—just a drop of milk and a few granules of sugar. She kept standing near me, watching me. When she took the cup she smiled and her legs rested against the armrest and my arm for more than a few seconds. I got up and took the cup back from her and put it on the table and hugged her. I kissed her all over her glossy face, but when it came to closing in on her lips, she avoided me. We moved towards the bedroom, my left arm round her waist and my right exploring her all over. She took her sari off but not her blouse and when I tried to unhook it she wriggled and laughed and prevailed. It was only after quite a few nights together that she finally took it off on her own. As we would go at it her smile would become more and more luminous by the moment till there was a sort of a sunburst at the climax. There was nothing very surreptitious about her coming. The butler would announce with a straight face that she would serve the coffee (which she always did) and that was it. She wouldn't take money. What made me smile was that compassion seemed to drip from her face when she was with me. Could that have motivated her? Even at work I would catch myself thinking of that brown glossy face, the velvet touch of her body, and her considerable passion.

I felt no guilt. Fidelity of course means the exclusion of the rest of the world. Now there was no one to be loyal to and hence none to be excluded on her count.

After some months, and they were good months, I found a slight bulge in her belly. For a month I didn't have the courage to ask her. (Conversation with her was not very elaborate in any case, because of the gulf between languages. It was more a dialogue of bodies. I may be putting it very crudely, but it was also a dialogue between two affections. She was never in a hurry to get away. We were both of us calm and unhurried, and we would talk now and then, I in my language and she in hers. I didn't want her to laugh at me when I spoke in her lingo.) By then there was no need to ask. I had been ruminating on what my next step should be. I would have let things drift, but then it was that my boss called me to the Calcutta office. Perhaps the rumour mills had got to him. I parted with her, leaving her, by her standards, or even by mine, a substantial amount of money.

And I sold the piano, and I presume the minuets and Liszt's *Hungarian Rhapsodies* went with it.

III. After the War

The euphoria of the victory was over. There wasn't much of it in any case. Euphoria can't last long if you have shortages—of gasoline and meat and milk and a lot of your young are dead. All the same I was sent to India to have a 'deco' as they say. The Northeast had been in a bad way, within an inch of being run over by the Japs, till they were stopped at Kohima. The Kohima battle was epic—not so much Slim versus Mutagachi, the two generals on either side, but because of the soldiers, who threw grenades at each other and fought hand to hand at the Deputy Commissioner's house. My partner's son was with the 4th Royal West Kent, which fought on the Ridge. He never tired of telling me about the wooded spur abutting on the Garrison Hill and how they fought the Japanese off with shovels and bayonets at the tennis courts! So did the Rajputs. And he never tired of quoting Mountbatten who called it, according to him, 'probably one of the greatest battles in history... the British/Indian Thermopylae'.

Well, all this had an effect on tea. The gardens had gone to weed—Cuthbert's certainly had. Conversely, I had made my way up; you always do if you just stick around. I was on the Board of Directors, and considered, to my embarrassment, as one of the few experts left in the tea world. (The others must have got shot up in the War!) I flew in to our Indian head office in ragged Calcutta, torn by sectarian friction. This was not the Calcutta I had known. The ravages of the Bengal famine, and the exodus into the metropolis it had triggered off, were visible, with hordes of people sleeping on pavements. I visited the firm's gardens in Darjeeling—anything to get away from Calcutta, and then landed in Dibrugarh. A month earlier someone had thrown a bomb here. Who would ever have thought of a thing like that in the late twenties? Christ, how could tea have turned political?

The town had grown, like all Indian towns—a wilderness of ugly houses and uglier shops moving out in all directions and making inroads into the bucolic Assam countryside. How contented that countryside looked—each little house with its clump of plantain trees and its fishpond. The Estate Manager received me, a Bengali gentleman called Sen. He was a thin, pleasant-faced man who carried himself well despite his bunched-up shoulders. My partner had called him 'Something Something Sen', but I had taken care in Calcutta to take down the name—Ashutosh. A bit of a tongue-twister that, but I had practised pronouncing it. The manager took me to the Circuit House. That means there still isn't a decent hotel in this dump, I reflected. But the view cheered me up, the Brahmaputra flowing by in all its grandeur. (One thing you had to say for the ICS, Imperial Civil Service, if you please. They may have fucked up the country, but they certainly sited their Inspection Houses rather well.) Over a cup of coffee I told Ashutosh, 'Do you mind if I call you Ash?' I didn't want any hiccups over the pronunciation. In my earlier stint in India I had learnt this lesson—never try to pronounce the unpronounceable.

Then followed a long chat about tea, the garden labour, and market and of course competition. I told him as gently as I could, hoping to soften the blow, that the Partners (and I was one of them) were even thinking of cutting losses and pulling out. Sell the damned thing and be done! But I was against any such move. Once this independence issue was resolved things would brighten up, or so I hoped. The war was over and economies had to bounce back the world over, not just in Assam. Running like an invisible thread through the whole discussion, which spilled over lunch, was this thought that went round my mind: why had Ash still not mentioned the bomb? Eventually my patience gave way and I asked directly, 'Let me know about the bomb.'

'Oh yes, the bomb. Well, someone threw it!'

That was very informative! He'd go on after that I thought, but Ash seemed to clam up as if no more need be said.

'Where exactly was it thrown?'

'Oh yes, in the glazed verandah, you remember, Sir, the one in the rear. But the fellow couldn't see that there was no one inside, I mean no one in the verandah.'

'The verandah was not glazed in my time. Were you in the house, when the bomb went off?'

'Oh yes, I was very much there. So was my wife, but no one was hurt.'

'Was it a powerful bomb?'

'Quite. Shards of broken glass were found a hundred yards away.'

'It just shattered glass, did it?'

'No, it smashed the wall in places, gouged a big hole there, if you ask me, a neat little hole with burn marks at the edges.'

'Who was it?'

'Who was what?'

'I mean who do you think did it?'

'I really wouldn't know. That's for the police to say.'

Why was Ash being cagey? 'Could it have been one of your workers?'

'No chance. Firstly there is no unrest among the labour. Moreover where could these Santhals have got hold of a bomb? This must have been political, but I really can't speculate on the matter. What I mean is, it wouldn't be informed speculation, if I could word it that way.'

It was time for him to take leave. As Ashutosh got up, he said rather casually, 'By the way, Sir, the Superintendent Police wanted to see you.'

'The SP? What on earth for?'

'I really don't have any idea.'

'How did he get to know I was here?'

'Well, the reservations in the Circuit House. The Collector and the SP get a list of people staying in here. In fact I have asked both of them to dinner tonight.'

'Are you sure? Is your house in shape, I mean have the repairs been carried out after the bomb?'

Styles had changed, I noticed at dinner, but still not as much as I had feared. It wasn't a sit-down affair. People trooped in a little late, including the Collector and no one seemed particularly apologetic. Instead of the one customary round of whisky or gin and lime there were two and at times three; some of the people could knock back a drink pretty fast. At the meal itself, while the roast was very much in prominence, I found too many curries, one looking like the other. The chatter too was political in all respects—what Gandhi and Jinnah were up to in Delhi or Bardoloi in Assam or that tongue-twister Fazl-ul-Haq in Calcutta. A few questions were thrown at me, perhaps out of politeness, about tea and England—rations, Attlee, football and of course cricket. Wally Hammond was touring Australia with the English side and getting a hammering. Bradman was out at 28, as everyone knew in England, caught by Ikin off Bedser, but didn't walk. And the bloke went on to make 187 and our woes started. I could have waxed eloquent on that one, except that the mood here was sombre. Politics is seldom fun. The SP, Jeremy White, stocky and square-shouldered, his cheeks red as fresh scabs, was outspoken.

'You can't run a country this way. Arrest the fellow today, release him tomorrow; make him Chief Minister the third day. You step out of jail into the cabinet and the Viceroy or the Governor swears you in. Then you step out of the cabinet into the jail. We don't even know how long *we* are going to be here. The country is on fire, we all know. That bum in Calcutta is holding a razor to the Hindu throat. And he's about to show the green light any day and watch the fun.' He passed his forefinger across his throat. 'Then just you watch how the blood runs.'

The doomsayers were clearly in a majority. I switched off for a while looking at the spot where the piano was once kept—and the *Hungarian Rhapsodies* that I fancied were locked in there. Where did this sudden yearning stem from, this intense desire to look at Pat again and hear her voice and listen to her piano. For months I may not have thought of her and now this doomed craving. As the plates were being cleared and the glasses brought out for the port (thank God Ash was keeping up the tradition) the SP moved over to my side. 'I believe you lived here once.'

'Well yes. It was a different house then. There was no glazed verandah, no portico and no bamboo fence—just a hibiscus hedge. That huddle of shops across the road was not there. We got some lovely evening breeze in the verandah. I don't know who got the thing covered and glazed.'

I got up and both of us moved over to the

verandah. He lit his cheroot, and when he took his first puff, I noticed the sense of satisfaction it seemed to give him. He must have felt cramped inside.

'I wish the verandah was not glazed. They'd have had less glass to break, I mean the chaps who threw the bomb.'

He drew on his cheroot at least three times while he spoke those two sentences.

'If they don't get glass they'll have other things to smash up, the terrorists.'

'I am not sure if they were terrorists. But we need to talk about that. Mr Campbell, Sir, I would like a word with you, when you have the time.'

'We could discuss whatever you have in mind right now, though I don't see how I can be of any interest to you.'

'I'd rather call on you tomorrow, if I may, Sir,' said the SP.

There was no way I could get out of this and agreed to the meeting.

'I could come at eight in the morning, if I may. I hope that's not too early?'

It was. The bugger won't even let me shit in peace, I thought. Could you make it ten, I said.

'Well, if eight's too early for you then ten it will be. Actually it is Friday tomorrow and I will be on the parade ground at six.'

I wasn't about to catch the hint. He could be at the parade ground at midnight, for all I cared. I certainly wouldn't have wanted him to stamp into the room in his boots and putties, the dust of the parade ground flaking over the carpet.

I wasn't looking forward to it; a meeting with a cop can never be all lilacs and lemons, if you ask me. The next morning, sharp at ten, Jeremy White was at the door. We got down to business straight away, after some tea. As the cups were taken away, he said, 'I must begin by saying that one has heard about you and your great record in the First War. You must be regretting that you were not the right age for the Second.' I didn't know why he brought that up. It looked like a century since I had been in the trenches. All the same I nodded in acknowledgement, hiding my slight surprise that

Jeremy White should have gone to such lengths to find things about me.

'You must be very concerned that a bomb should have been thrown at your manager's house, the same house you lived in once. It was a fairly powerful bomb and Sen and his wife were lucky to escape. Damned lucky if you ask me. He was a bit foolhardy in rushing out and hollering like mad after it had gone off. If the chap who hurled the bomb had a pistol he could have shot him. Anyway the hollering helped matters because people ran to the house and some of them chased the fellow.'

'The terrorist?'

'We are not fully certain that he *was* one. He was very athletic and out-sped his pursuers. But people managed to see him, and everyone said he was white. "Gora, gora," they all said. We were obviously intrigued. Was it someone with leucoderma? we thought first. Could it be an Anglo-Indian? We kept vigil at the bus stands and the railway station through the night. We raided hotels and dharmashalas. In the morning we got lucky. I thought of the tug, the steamboat, which plies along the Brahmaputra. We sent a guard of four scrambling to the bank. And believe it or not one fellow jumped into the water. The trouble was he was swimming with the current and the ferry was going the other way. By the time the guard prevailed upon the Ferry Master to turn the boat around, the fellow had disappeared. The bullets fired from those .410 muskets weren't up to much. He escaped but again the passengers swore that though the fellow was all wrapped up in a shawl and a muffler, the little they saw of him told them he was white. Some even claimed that he had disguised himself and painted his face black. The first definite information we had on the fellow was when our raids at these religious guest houses, dharmashalas as they call them, bore fruit. The chap at the Jain Guest House said there were three of them and one of them was white. He didn't like the looks of them and had also warned them not to eat meat on the premises. We scoured the riverbanks but he seemed to have got away. He hadn't. Eventually we got him, floundering through the hills, quite a few miles from here. He had hurt his knee badly when he had swum away from the ferry.'

I still couldn't understand what all this was leading to. Why is the man telling me all this? 'What did the man say when he was caught?'

'Not much, I am afraid. We have strict orders that political suspects should be treated with kid gloves. We haven't been able to get even the names of his companions out of him. But the Calcutta police has helped us with names.'

'Mr White, did he have anything against Sen?'

'Not that I know of. But he does seem to have been spurred on by a lot of hate.'

'What kind? He hated planters, did he? Did his people ever work in the gardens?'

'I was coming to that. He hates a single individual. Actually he was born in one of the outhouses in Sen's compound.'

White waited to see if that bit of news had any effect on me, but I am certain there wasn't a flicker on my face though I had started feeling a bit uneasy. 'But that must have been a while before Sen came in.'

'Quite. After you came Bates, then Lindsay, then Watford—he stayed for seven years, and then came the Indians. Actually he was born in the outhouses somewhere around your time, or maybe a little after.'

'As far as I remember, and it's twenty years or so mind you, no one was born in the outhouses while I was here.'

'I don't know how to say this, Mr Campbell, but what little we got out of him—his name is Vikram by the way—was that he had a personal vendetta against you.'

'Me! Why on earth?' I tried to look a little puzzled and am sure I succeeded.

'We thought you'd be able to tell us.'

'Mr White, he was born after I left. We never could have met. Right?'

'That's right.'

What was the fellow getting at in that case? And what did he expect me to tell him? Or was he just trying to turn the tourniquet?

'Then where could the question of vendetta come in, Mr White? Even if he had some imaginary grudge, so damned what? And you keep saying you are not sure if he was a terrorist. Well, if he wasn't then how on earth did he get hold of a bomb? Couldn't have been a Christmas gift, for sure.'

'I am not in any way seeking an alibi for him, Mr Campbell, Sir. He is a blackguard, no doubt about that—black heart in white sheath.'

The fellow needed a put-down. A skylight needed to be opened in the dark cabin of his mind. 'M. White, these people are fighting for freedom. When you fight for freedom, you...fight, damn it; you shed blood. How many people do we know of who have fought for independence without shedding blood, their own and that of the people who rule over them?'

He didn't know what to say. He looked surprised that I seemed to be taking their side. 'All the same, Mr Campbell, I have his photograph here. I thought you'd like to see it.' I noticed a smirk (which he made no attempt to hide) on his boiled-beetroot face.

It was faintly familiar, the photograph, and it took me a second to learn why. He looked quite like me. I handed it back. 'Did he tell you the cause of this so-called grudge of his?'

'I am afraid not,' he said. Then why was the bastard wasting my time? 'He dropped a hint that he hated his white colour.'

'Oh, white rag to the bull, was it? Then he could have had a grouse against any Englishman.' I looked him squarely in the face, daring him to say a thing. He tried one last gambit—a cop will do anything to embarrass you.

'We still have the fellow on remand. I could have him brought here in a van. Would you want that?'

He was getting predictable now. I could hear that gnat buzzing in the glass jar of his brain. I look down upon see-through brains.

'I wouldn't, Mr White. I don't see what all this has to do with me. And I haven't come all the way from London to look into this bomb case. That's your job. And if you can't do it, I don't see why I should be roped into it.'

He got up, gave me one of his smarmy smirks, shook hands and took his leave.

Bird Island

He wouldn't tell his host that it was in a way the tenth anniversary. All the fun would go out of the trip. His wife never forgot the day, and never refrained from reminding him of the day her son had vanished.

His host, the nawab of Shamasabad, as fine a gentleman as ever there was, had prepared this excursion with considerable care. He had got his guns oiled and cleaned with a rag. And he had stocked enough twelve-bore cartridges to shoot each denizen of a game reserve, leave alone a duck shoot in the wetlands known as *khadir* here.

The guns, he noticed, were the best in the line,

a James Purdey and two Holland-and-Hollands. The butt of one the guns had inlay work on it and the other had a mother-of-pearl coat. When he held them he was amazed how light they were. The nawab was a bit embarrassed when asked if they were custom made. (For, in that case, the price would be sky high.) Yes they were, he said reluctantly, and then his ten-year-old nephew showed Sudhakar the one meant for deer and boar shoots and the one for birds.

He realized he was a novice. He had always thought that guns were the same, it was the cartridges, rather the pellets in the cartridges, which defined the target. Yes, tigers and leopards would need a different weapon, one could imagine, but the others?

Logistics were left to his friend's friend, Colonel Majumdar. Sudhakar was told that the colonel was meticulous about details. The boat would be his. Sudhakar was a bit reluctant to tell the nawab that he had of late lost the appetite for going after game, big or small.

'Where exactly are we headed tomorrow,

Nawab Sahib?' Though they had been friends for ages, the mode of address was always formal from both sides. Of course, you couldn't address royalty by first name. And royalty itself was so polite, the manners so impeccable, that you almost felt out of sorts.

'Don't worry, we are boating along the Ramganga, downstream of course. We'll be up much before dawn since we have to drive at least thirty miles to the river. The road, as you saw this morning, isn't too good.'

Sudhakar didn't feel like riddling the taciturn, slightly rotund nawab with a salvo of questions. They had been to the same school, though the nawab had been there some years earlier. Still, it was a bond of sorts. He had retired from his job and the nawab had asked him to come.

Twenty years ago, the nawab and he had fished in the Gomti together. Earlier the nawab had come with a baraat and he had been asked by the bride's father to 'entertain' the nobleman. That's how they had got to know each other. The hills were his beat and Sudhakar had invited him later to fish for trout in the Pindar. And they had trekked together.

The nawab looked soft, but he could walk a good fifteen miles a day, and he didn't flinch or look tired in the evening.

Absence can be heavy; it can weigh you down. It had made Sudhakar's shoulders droop for over ten years now. His son had walked out on them and there was no way they could find him. 'Not the police,' his wife Hemlata had said. She was afraid of the courts and the black-robed ones, whether on the bench or the bar. Her father had been caught in a land dispute with his cousins, in cases and appeals that had gone on for years. Litigation under the law the British had left us with was a sort of a *chakravyuha*, a roll of barbed wire in which you got entangled for life. 'He could have come under a truck,' Sudhakar had suggested to his wife one day, and she had refused to speak to him for a week.

She had been visiting astrologers, believed in sadhus and holy mantras of not-so-holy men. A havan had been organized in the house, wood-fire and ghee and a tonsured pujari with a hoarse voice—and of course, white sheets spread on the floor. A red thread had been sanctified by prayer and then tied round his wrist. That much he had allowed on his wife's insistence. He had no time for pandit and pujari, had cultivated distaste for saffron and ochre, these supposedly spiritual signposts. But what can you do but humour your wife who has lost her son?

The son Sukhdeo had always been too quiet—speech had landed on the child's tongue after he had crossed the age of three. Did he have enough friends in college, his parents had kept wondering. He stayed in his room upstairs on the second floor—just his room and the wide windy terrace lined with flower pots. Of course, there was a TV antenna fixed there—even though TV and its Doordarshan avatar were new to the country. They had given him a small set but he never switched it on, or almost never. He had his tape deck though and played his Kishori Amonkars frequently.

Sudhakar avoided going up and prying.

Hemlata would egg him on. 'See what he's up to? Can't you do even that?'

'Let him have his privacy,' he would tell her.

'What privacy! What privacy from father and mother! He should be sitting with us and chatting or going out with friends. I wouldn't mind if he got drunk somewhere, and beat up someone, or got beaten up. Even a brawl would be better than this clo-cloi—what is the word?'

'Cloistered living, you wanted to say.'

She would nod. He had a knack of knowing what she wanted to say, rather where she got stuck.

He'd shake his head in disbelief. 'He is a brooder.'

'What is that supposed to mean?' she'd ask, agitated.

'He broods.'

'You say this so matter-of-factly, as if it was the naturalest thing in the world to brood! *Wah*!' Her grammar went awry when her temper rose.

He'd just shrug—the best gesture invented to date when faced with angry wives.

He had asked her one day—that was two years

after their son disappeared—if what had happened to her father was the only reason why she resisted going to the 'authorities'.

Yes, it was, she had said.

But he had seen her eyes turn evasive and her lips quiver.

He had persisted.

She eventually came out with it. What if the police confirmed their worst fears? What if they dug out the bones of some buried jackal and said, these are your son's skeletal remains?

He had tried to allay her fears. She was being paranoid, he had told her, and then couldn't resist an aside—no one buries jackals.

She had lost her temper. 'You know damn well what I mean. I don't mean the police will hand me bones of a jackal or dog or hyena. Even I know that. Some beggar's bones, some unclaimed dead body lying in the mortuary...'

He didn't say a thing, though he had felt like telling her they wouldn't do a thing like that.

She quietened down and then with considerable effort had said, 'Suppose Sukhdeo is dead and they confront me with that?'

He had no answer. When facts turn brutal, not many people want to face them.

She had hinted at irrefutable proof—clothes and things, the gold chain he always wore, the two strands of that sanctified red thread which were wound around his left wrist also.

They got into the nawab's two-coloured Chevrolet at first light. It was then that Sudhakar summoned up the courage to tell him that now his shooting was restricted to the camera shutter. He would not like to carry that Holland-and-Holland, honoured though he was. He had held it once and just the feel of it had sent a thrill through him. But a resolve was a resolve. For years, he hadn't touched a gun. If the nawab was disappointed or surprised at his friend's reaction, he didn't show it. He just smiled benevolently and let it go at that.

They drove to the Ramganga, the river which divided the districts of Farrukhabad and Shahjahanpur. On each bank he could see a swathe of sand, now and then pockmarked with patches of grass. The boat was there, and Colonel Majumdar who commanded the Rajputana Rifles, or Raj-Rifs in army slang. The boat was decked with a rug and a cushion to sit on; there were two rowers in army fatigues and a mess aabdar in turban and achkan to serve breakfast and then beer. His paraphernalia, which included a primus stove, was spread over one corner of the boat.

The colonel had thought of everything. There were even straw hats to shield his guests from the winter sun later in the day.

Colonel Majumdar, a genial moustachioed man, had his own gun. They started rowing upriver. The nawab introduced Majumdar as a fast bowler in his young days. Sudhakar, a keen cricketer himself, exchanged some stories with him. The colonel told them how he had got Pataudi caught in the slips in the first innings. But in the second, the man stood a yard out of the crease and smashed Majumdar all over the park.

The sun was up now and he saw a gull almost resting on the water and for a moment dreaded that the boat would go over and smother it. Sudhakar looked down and saw the gull's image plummeting into the river even as it rose. He wondered if he had got them on camera, both bird and image. He would develop the film in his darkroom. The sight, unforgettable as it was, forgotten for the moment. His thoughts focused on whether the bird would be clear and sharp and its image in the water aqueous, almost mystical. He started wondering if all that was mystic wasn't slightly smudged, and if haze and the mystical could be said to be of the same ilk. He was woken up from his reverie when he heard the sound of laughter; the colonel and the nawab were in splits.

'Where were you?' asked the colonel.

'In my darkroom,' he answered. He proceeded to educate them about his darkroom, his sophisticated camera, the wide-angle lens and why he developed his own films.

They passed lowing cattle, cowherds clicking their tongues as they moved to the grazing grounds. A bird went up and he thought of a receding ellipse.

Breakfast time: The aabdar had tea ready by now and was serving it along with sandwiches. The nawab murmured that the birds would hear the clatter of fork and plate, cup and saucer. Sudhakar saw a few birds flying away, but thought nothing of it, his mind occupied with omelette and toast and the tea he was drinking.

Breakfast over, the two shikaris with him readied their guns. They could hear the squawk of the birds now.

'We are nearing the river island,' whispered the colonel, finger on his lips to signal silence. A beautiful bird, its plumage resplendent, flew up but the nawab let it go. Too beautiful, he said, and added that it was a surkhab, a sheldrake. The river was getting noisier, for the mud island had divided the river into channels, and the flow grew louder and more rapid as they strained up the eastern strait. The colonel and the nawab now readied their guns at the shoulder, though they were still at a distance from the island.

All of a sudden, they saw the whole island rise up in front of them, as if some bird god had summoned the entire waterfowl kingdom to the skies. It was a shock for Sudhakar—a thousand water birds, murghaab and kaaz, geese, grebe and mallard, swamp hen and tern rising like some gigantic cloud, bird cloud, squawking and screaming and cackling during this winged lift-off. Many of the birds were wet. Light shimmered as it alighted on their backs only to slip off, as if it had glanced off shards of galvanized steel. All three of them were stunned by the scene, this vast latticework of wings moving ahead to the accompaniment of the cacophony of bird cries.

'They bring the north here every winter, isn't it?' asked the nawab rather philosophically.

'Yes, they must be wondering why they took the trouble to come here, flying a thousand miles, if they were to be chased out.' That was Sudhakar's contribution. A flock of waterfowl circled around and flew off on cue, their cries sounding a bit querulous, as if they were asking what kind of an island was this with guns on the lookout.

They were now alongside the island and the colonel asked if they would want to alight. Both Sudhakar and the nawab declined. They noticed a straw hut on the far side of the island and suddenly a man appeared on the scene. He was hunkering down and now he stood up. He was bearded and had a stick in his hand. Even from the distance he seemed to be in a poor state, more apparition than man.

The nawab shook his head. 'I don't think we will get many birds today.'

Why must you be pessimistic, chided the colonel.

The nawab did not reply.

'Who could that man be?' asked Sudhakar. He had pointed his camera at the man but thought he was too far away.

'A hobo probably. The down-and-outs choose peculiar places.'

The nawab agreed with the colonel. 'The man could be off his nut.'

Sudhakar kept talking about him, still wondering who he could be, why the birds had crowded the island despite him being there. Why on earth were they not frightened of him?

The birds had now settled on the banks, but they had seen the boat and were keeping an eye on it. Each time they were within gunshot, they flew away. Each time the nawab shook his head.

Meanwhile the beer bottles had been opened and the liquid poured into the glistening tankards bearing the insignia of the regiment. The nawab was having none of it, he never touched alcohol.

'With all this activity we won't get a thing,' the nawab remarked yet again. 'A month back, I came here on bullock cart and travelled along the bank. I shot twenty birds.'

Sudhakar was not having a bad day, though. His camera had kept clicking.

The river shimmered under the sun. They decided to circle the island now and return along the other bank. As they neared the straw hut they saw what they had so far been calling the apparition. He was wearing a sort of robe of cotton twill. It was dirty and old. His face was sun-blackened, the cheeks hollow and the beard shaggy. They observed his falter-walk as he moved towards the boat. Sudhakar couldn't resist his curiosity and said he would like to get onto the island. His pretence was that he would get a good shot with his camera. They all got down. The apparition moved towards them.

'Where are you from and why are you living on this island?' asked the colonel kindly.

'If one's needs are few, one can live anywhere he wants, sahib.'

Sudhakar was startled. He felt unreal, he didn't know why.

'But why here?' persisted the colonel. 'Why on this island with the birds?'

'The birds don't trouble me. I don't trouble them.'

'What is your name?'

'What has a name got to do with it, sahib? One lives with the river-wind and the river, with bird and fish, and with silence, with the seasons and the night.'

Sudhakar had stood rooted so far. Something touched a memory nerve, the gait, the voice. He staggered a bit and couldn't get the words out of his mouth. The nawab caught him by the arm, but he gently shook him off and advanced towards the birdman.

'Sukhdeo?' he said, looking intently at the man and advancing towards him, hope shining like two torchlights from his eyes.

The birdman's face lit up.

Daughter

It was still about two hours to midnight. Ardeshir was at his prayers, a black velvet skull-cap on his head and the double-stranded sacred thread held loose in his hands. His feet were planted about two feet from each other and he was swaying from side to side as he mumbled his prayers, the weight of the body shifting from one leg to the other almost rhythmically. As he intoned the names of the three hells of the Zoroastrian Cosmos—Dushmata, Duzukhta, Duzvarshta, he lashed the air with the sacred thread the way one snaps a whip to egg on a lazy cart horse. When you mention Satan (Ahriman) or one of the hells he reigns in, some action indicative of strong disapproval must accompany the mouthing of the name. A medieval Assize passing sentence on a witch or a heretic could not have done so with greater vehemence. In his condemnation of evil, Zoroaster was as severe as the semitic prophets who followed. Fire and brimstone. But when Ardeshir intoned the name of the good Lord Ahura Mazda, he took the sacred thread respectfully to his eyeballs. He lifted his shirt-hem, holding it fast with his chin against his chest as he tied his prayer-knots, one in front at the navel and the other on the tailbone. That done, the shirt-hem fell in place and the side-to-side rocking started once again. Another fifteen minutes and the prayers were over. Ardeshir bent his arthritic back and touched the ground three times with his fingers in homage to a painting of Zoroaster hung on the wall in front. The salutation took in also the cotton wick, which sputtered with flame in a small glass containing oil, burning under the photograph of his dead son. The oil lamp, the photograph and the prayer book, *Khordeh Avesta*, were all placed on a corner table. Over it loomed the stylized portrait of the Prophet, his muslin garments fluttering as if he was standing in front of a pedestal fan, a trident in his left hand and the forefinger of the right hand held aloft to proclaim that there was only one God. One could almost date the things portrayed. Those folds of gauze-like muslin in which Zoroaster was wrapped came in obviously after the eighth-century migration to India. The forefinger came in after the passionate monotheism of Islam. And that blond beard obviously after the English had conquered India. So there you were, half the history of the Orient recorded in a swatch of paint.

The prayers over, Ardeshir devoted himself to the closing of doors and the fastening of windows of their Sundernagar house. Each evening he supervised this operation hovering next to their domestic, Shyam Singh. And once Shyam Singh left, the ritual started again, each window being put through close scrutiny. Were the upper and the lower latches embedded firmly in their slots? Was the bathroom door properly closed? Half the thefts occurred through the bathroom. A skylight or a window left open for the night, and all the man had to do was to force the bars wide enough for a slim person to slip in. Then if the door to the bedroom was not bolted from the other side, you were in trouble. He never ceased to worry at this phenomenon. Out in the night the biggest thieves, crooks, kidnappers, rapists could be prowling around sticking their knives into people, or hopefully, into each other. But here, encircled by the four walls of your house, with every door latched and all the fastenings in place, you were as secure as the crown jewels in the Tower. That was what civilization was all about. The men who first rolled a large stone to the cave-mouth and slept peacefully had no idea that they were actually ushering in civilization itself. The wheel, writing, air flights, Mr Nixon and condoms would all follow. But once someone gained entry inside, it was as good as being sold to the devil. You were then in the clutches of naked evil. It could do what it liked with you, beat you with a rubber hose, force out your nails or set fire to your hair. Rendered powerless and impotent, you could merely watch a fount of satanic evil erupt in front of you. When people said their prayers at night they were perhaps thanking the Lord for everything. Fathomless satisfaction, that is what most people suffered from. And then an agent of evil got inside and their worlds collapsed about them in a way their cramped spirits could never have imagined. These very four walls then made you more vulnerable for now you could not break out, while evil prowled inside with its daggers unsheathed.

It was July now and the big desert cooler was in disuse, and the water had been drained from the tank. Now and then for an hour or so Ardeshir switched the exhaust on to blow the cool night air inside. Dressed in his white pyjamas and his muslin vest he started walking up and down in the verandah after switching off the light. He walked barefoot, a spectral wisp of a shadow moving across the windows lit up spasmodically by bars of the distant street light that fell in faintly luminous stripes across the windows.

His bed creaked as it received him. It too was getting old, he thought. As for him, he would be joining the ranks of the *nouveaux pauvres* the next year, when he retired. The climbdown from one's salary to living on the monthly interest of your Provident (and how provident!) Fund was considerable. But in a way he was impatient for the day and wanted to be done with it. For the last five years he had started calculating time backwards from the date of his retirement. There was something unnatural and retrograde in the clockhands moving backwards. It was akin to a reversal of the season cycle. All that would end, this time-spool running backwards once he retired. Or would it? Wouldn't his imagination, now habituated to cut-off dates, start counting backwards from some vaguely notional death-date?

His wife Firoza's face was a bit puffed up in the morning, as if some blister fly had bitten her just under the eyes. He overheard her talking to their daughter in an inaudible, low-key murmur. He heard her opening the lock of a wall cupboard in their room and rummaging among the clothes. He knew what that meant. Arnavaz must have had her period. Once that happened she was to wear only a shirt and a pair of jeans laid aside just for this. Also a skirt which he had come to recognize, a flaring knee-length skirt with blazing floral prints which had been handed down from the wide hips of her aunt Beroz. He also knew the two frayed night dresses set apart for her during her 'time', as Parsee women would put it. Come to think of it, the usage was not really off mark. In fact it was quite close to what the Americans would call doing time. Because with the onset of the period a hundred taboos descended on the woman. She could sit only on one particular chair, made of aluminium piping, eat in one particular plate made of steel, and sleep on an old iron bed with iron springs. Metal could not be defiled. Once the period was over she was to shampoo her hair and change into normal clothes. There was also a change of linen in the room. Only books, schoolbags and her tennis racket remained unchanged, immune to pollution.

Still, at breakfast he absent-mindedly asked Arnavaz to fetch his specs and the Sunday paper. She made no move as if she had not heard him and Firoza glared at him disapprovingly, the eyelids opening wide for a flickering fraction of a moment. Though paper and glasses could not be polluted, he should not have asked her. He pushed his chair back and got up slowly, walked to the front door, bent down and picked the paper up from under the door leaves. Holding his left hand to his lumber region, he got up and walked back slowly to the table.

It was then that he glanced casually at her feet and noticed with surprise that she had been neglecting her nail polish. He remembered how only some years back Firoza had insisted on painting her toe-nails barely an hour before being admitted into the hospital for her tubectomy. And frugal as she was, every once in a while she walked into a beauty clinic (no one called them saloons any more, he wondered) for a manicure. At the moment the nails were an unwholesome white, both at the edges and near the cuticle. There must be something very seriously wrong, he thought, to have made her neglect herself in this manner.

Leaving Bombay had been his original sin. That at least was what Firoza thought. To leave Bombay and the community, the whist parties at the Dadar Parsee Gymkhana, the bhelpuri at Chaupati and the odd ice cream at the Parsee Dairy Farm was unthinkable. She was nostalgic for those sacred thread ceremonies at the Colaba Fire-Temple and those weddings at the All Bless Baug. Parsee weddings, if you please, where you displayed your heirloom diamonds and rubies; not those Marwari affairs where you were weighed down with maunds of gold, looking for all the world like a bullion market. Wedding feasts where you tucked in enough to last you a week, not just the chicken and the steamed coconut-and-coriander fish and the chips-and-meat with its thick, spicy gravy, but also fried eggs! And you topped it off with a custard. That was perhaps the first dessert the Parsees learnt from the English and it had become the traditional wedding dessert.

To have left Bombay for Poona or Lonavla or Karjat was one thing. But to leave your house and bank in Bombay and to come and live with the Punjabis in Delhi! That was madness. In the five years he had been in Delhi, Ardeshir (Adi to his friends) Bilimoria thought he discerned a substratum of reproach in probably every word his wife spoke to him.

It was a hot and sticky July morning. Arnavaz had put on her salwar-kameez after her bath and he found her standing in front of the mirror busy with her cosmetics. He walked over to Firoza. 'Where's she going in this heat?' he asked, conscious of a querulous note creeping into his voice.

'Why don't you ask her?' Ten minutes later, Firoza stopped abruptly in front of him during one of her visits to and from the kitchen.

'So you didn't ask her. Courage deserted you, as it always does, when it comes to speaking to your daughter. Not one unpleasant question will you risk, will you? Every harsh word must come from me!'

After a minute's pause during which she opened the refrigerator, took out a milk jug and placed a few eggs in a bowl, she said, 'And I will tell you where she has gone. She has gone to Anwar!'

'Did she tell you that?'

'She did not. As if she tells me anything!' She stomped into the kitchen, her heels pounding on the floor. An hour later he tried to appease her even though he read the storm signs on her face, lips quivering and eyes on the brink of tears.

'There's no need to spring to conclusions,' he said soothingly, trying hard to keep irritation away from his voice. 'How can you be certain where she's gone and with whom? Even if she's gone to meet Anwar—'

'So what? That's what you were going to say isn't it?'

'That's not what I was going to say,' he said, trying hard to get a grip over himself and keep his temper. 'I wish you wouldn't interrupt. What I was going to say is there could be a perfectly harmless reason for meeting Anwar.'

'Such as?' she let the question hang in the air. He noticed her lips, two horizontal cracks of sarcasm that separated the well-fleshed face from the small mouth.

'I can't tell you off-hand, but it could be anything. She could have gone to return a book, for instance.' He started feeling a little less sure of himself. 'There can be a hundred reasons why one human being meets another,' he added forcefully. What he lacked in certitude he made up for with vehemence.

'Wouldn't you like to be certain, Ardeshir? Wouldn't you like to ask Arnavaz whether she went out with Anwar? A specific question, mind you, looking her right in the eyes, not a vague enquiry with your eyes peering sideways or downwards as if it is you who's guilty.'

'Nobody is guilty, Firoza! Your imagination is running away with you.'

She had obviously had enough by now.

'When one fine day somebody runs away with your daughter, and a Muslim at that, then I'll see who talks about guilt. Then guilt will hang around your neck like a...a stone.' She had wanted to say 'millstone' but the word did not come to her readily and because of the lunch she was cooking, the word which had naturally surfaced was 'grindstone'. She was speaking with the kind of intensity that did not come easily to her. Years of disillusion and indifference had left their sediment-layers on her soul. One could not go to the extent of saying that their marriage was fraying at the seams, but mutual respect had certainly become a casualty of advancing years. He looked down on the pettiness of her concerns. She in turn despised the paucity of will in him.

Anwar came from Pathan stock, had studied in Delhi and landed a good job with Grindlay's Bank. Arnavaz had met him at parties at the houses of her father's banking colleagues. Ardeshir was the manager of a Central Bank branch. He had nothing against Anwar. He was fair and good-looking though not as tall as Pathans are. He had a low, modulated voice and could speak knowledgeably on many things, including music. Sitting alongside Arnavaz on a settee he had talked about Zahrin Daruwalla and her sarod. Arnavaz had heard the name, but that was all. If it came to the crunch she would have been hard put to distinguish between a sarod and a sitar or any other Indian string instrument. But when she switched the conversation to western music she found him speaking authoritatively on everything from jazz and blues to Bach and Mahler. And he spoke with such warmth. What a change from her careworn, taciturn father, and her mother, who for quite some time had been estranged from all pleasures, stronger on prohibitions than on enthusiasms.

Ardeshir was determined to confront Arnavaz on her return. He had to show the wife that he could be firm when he wanted. As usual, Arnavaz walked straight into her room, got hold of a book and plonked herself on the bed, tossing aside her sandals rather impatiently. Standing at the door he asked her, 'Where did you go?' He wanted to sound casual, but tension broke through his voice. Arnavaz kept on reading her book.

'Did you go to Anwar?' She lowered the book slightly so that she could look him in the eye, and then raised the book again.

'Did you go out with him somewhere? To a movie or something?'

She put her book down now, looking at him impassively as a jellyfish.

'Come on, I'm waiting for an answer!'

'Oh Papa!' she said. Then the doorbell rang. The neighbour wanted to telephone. And that was it. He never could bring himself to take up the subject with her again.

In the evening he took a walk by himself. From his house in Sundernagar he strolled down Cornwallis Road, starting from the remnants of the Old Fort, those disjointed mausoleum-like buildings inhabited by bats and echoes and horse-dung, and ending up at the Lodhi Gardens. But he had no eye for landscape today. His mind had got swamped with that one overwhelming question—what would happen if Arnavaz lost her heart to this Anwar? Some of his Parsee confrères would laugh their silly heads off, he thought. He had always been liberal-minded and, what was worse, had acquired this kind of a reputation. And his interest in Islam had always been pronounced. He remembered the occasion when someone had mentioned Islam and fanaticism in the same breath. He had rushed to the ramparts, swords out, as it were. It was the crusaders who were fanatics, he shouted. It was the likes of Richard *coeur de lion* and his myrmidons in their clanking chain mail, wielding their two-handed broadswords and all their talk about the 'heathen

Soldan' (that was Saladin, if you please) which had evoked this irrepressible urge to survive and convert to Islam. It was as logical as the workings of nature, he remembered to have said. If one thousandth or, in some cases, one millionth of a larvae survived, it ensured the survival of a species. Look at the over-insurance involved. So the Arabs proselytized. It was as simple as that.

Then there was the time his aunt and uncle had come from Karachi. His aunt had passed some derogatory remarks about the Arabs and gone on to say that it was from the Persians that the crescent caught its glory. He was appalled. He wasn't going to take this lying down. He harangued her for half an hour on the splendours of Jerusalem, Constantinople, Cordova, the massive Dome of the Rock with its intricate calligraphy, the mosaics from the great Umayyad mosque at Damascus. He talked of the Arabs and the Turks, the efflorescence of their culture, their mathematicians, astronomers, physicians, poets. He rattled off the tongue-twisting names, Al-Khawarizmi, one of the founders of Algebra, Al-Kindi, who as far back as the ninth century ridiculed alchemy, Abu Rhan Alberuni, who discovered that light travels faster than sound. But it was when he spoke of the Moor poets of Andalusia that his eyes lit up and he noticed his uncle and aunt making visible efforts to suppress a smile. It all came back. What would they say now?

That is what a little learning does to you, he reflected bitterly. Immediately people of your own ilk start giving you queer looks, as if you are, what the Americans call, an oddball. If you were as blinkered as the others, no one bothered. You were a part of a group and your own attitude became a part of a group prejudice, patina-work on a larger mosaic.

He realized with a slight jolt that he had crossed Humayun Road, which branched off to the right of the road he was walking on, without even looking out for any possible traffic. He got hold of himself and noticed pedestrians, cars, scooters for the first time, as also the mosque protruding onto the sidewalk. He had the eerie feeling of having been flung from a limbo into the heart of the screaming world. He had never felt so vulnerable as at this moment, with all his sense perceptions suddenly under attack.

At Sujan Singh Park he was handed over a leaflet by a college student. 'Rise to support the struggle of the Fighting Masses and Students of Iran', said the leaflet in thick black print. It talked of fifteen thousand people having died due to the bombing of residential areas in Kurdistan. 'The bombers attacked the Turkman Peasants Soviets last month and then the anti-people army and the Islamic Guards let terror loose in Turkman Sahara and executed thirty revolutionary Turkmans.' As he read the leaflet, standing on the pavement, Ardeshir found his thoughts wandering back to a lecture he had attended in the Birla Auditorium in Bombay in 1979. Ardeshir was spending his annual leave in town when an Associate Professor of Iranian Studies from Columbia had come and lectured on 'A Western Response to Zarathushtra'. He had talked of evil presenting itself to Zoroaster in a stark and naked form. Zoroaster had called this *Aesma*, akin to the Persian *Keshm*, which means fury. In the Zand Avesta, this violence, fury, evil, call it what you will, had been referred to as '*Aesma* of the bloody club'. The professor had gone on to say that in our own day the epithet could be substituted for '*Aesma* of the summary trial and the firing squads'. After the lecture, when it came to questions, Ardeshir had twice raised his arm but he somehow never caught the speaker's eye. All he had wanted to ask the American professor was why he had not mentioned the *Aesma* of the Savak torture chambers.

He walked back. There was no point in walking further to the Lodhi Gardens, he thought, when with each step his mind was getting more agitated. An evening stroll was supposed to bring you peace. Instead, all kinds of thoughts were whirling across his mind. He walked back, vaguely aware of two iceberg fears trying to surface into his consciousness. The first was his dread of confronting Firoza on the subject of Arnavaz. The second was the dread of living with his self-contempt if Arnavaz did marry Anwar. Even as the names ran across his mind he became aware that they sounded like two bells forged in the same smithy. God seemed to have made them for one another, connecting the names by assonantal chimes. But no, this couldn't happen; not to him, nor to his daughter with that flawless face of hers unmarked by either a mole or a pimple, and with a voice that sounded like a cello. This much he was certain of. If he could not stop this marriage he would despise himself till his dying day. An old age given up to cultivating self-contempt as you nurture an orchid, he reflected wryly.

The next week was given over to the planning of his strategy. She has only to be told about the quandary the community finds itself in. A community of just over a hundred thousand people, diminishing by ten thousand every decade. A casualty rate of a thousand a year, caused by celibacy, late marriages, sterility, inbreeding. And this was not happening to some head-hunters in Papua New Guinea or some rickets-afflicted tribe in the jungles of the Amazon. The remnants of one of the oldest civilizations were slowly dying without as much as a whimper. The spawn of the Magi, the practitioners of the fire-cult just embering away into nothingness like a cigar stub. He had only to put this into the right words and he was sure it would stoke the fires of her imagination. It would instil a sense of belonging in her. And the saga of their defeat, how within three decades of having reached the gates of Constantinople the Persians tasted defeat at their own door! And the conversions, that would surely fire her with vengeance against the conquerors.

He waited for the right day to broach the subject. The right day somehow never seemed to come. Strange as it may sound, no scrap of conversation ever led to Yezdegard, the seventh-century Parsee king who lost to the Arabs! After the wife and the daughter had gone to sleep Ardeshir would start his agitated walk up and down the enclosed verandah, thinking of ways and means to shore up the crumbling dyke of Zoroastrianism. Up and down he would go, his loose pyjamas making a swishing sound, his eyes luminous with the night-traffic of thoughts flitting past, his hands gesticulating and his lips mumbling in perpetual dialogue with his gestures.

Eventually he took a day's leave. That was

the only way he simply *would* have to talk to her, whether on cue or otherwise. Arnavaz was a little surprised to see him still in his pyjamas at breakfast, but apart from a momentary raising of her eyebrows there was no other reaction. She put her head down, quietly ate her omelette and walked into her room. A little later he followed her.

'A time comes when a child...' he cleared his throat here, 'a child, err, must know the history of her race. Racial attitudes, customs, racial memories are all moulded by history.' It sounded like the start of an essay or a prepared speech to Arnavaz, who, as usual, was reclining on her bed reading a book. Since appearing for her law exams she was doing nothing, just waiting for her results. He plunged in. 'Have you any idea what happened to the people of Iran when they fell to the sword and to Islam?' Arnavaz was in no mood to oblige him with an answer. She just kept looking at him impassively. 'Well, you must first know that it was all preordained. Yezdegard, the Iranian king, marched his troops to the borders of his kingdom on hearing of the intended Arab invasion. The Arab commander,

Mosanna, retreated. But a deputation of Muslims arrived and was summoned by the king to his presence. To make conversation, Yezdegard asked the Muslims what they called cloaks, whips and sandals in their language. The reply was *burd*, *saut* and *n'al*. The sound of the words was so ominous, for they bore a close resemblance to the Persian words for taking (*burden*), burning (*sukhtan*) and lamenting (*nalidan*) that the courtiers visibly paled. On being further questioned the leader of the deputation offered the king a choice between conversion to Islam or payment of tribute to the Arabs. The Persian king could not keep his cool. Dubbing them savages, he berated them for the food they took ("serpents and mice are your diet") and criticized them for their sartorial habits ("you have nothing to cover yourself with excepting the wool of camels and sheep"). "Of all the world's nations," he told them, "you are the scurviest, the poorest, the most ignorant, the most estranged from the arts. The dissensions in Persia must have really emboldened you to think of conquering us!" A little loftily Yezdegard offered to give them food and raiment in case "misery and want have driven you from your deserts". But the Arab leader was adamant. The choice before the king lay between accepting Islam or paying tribute. In anger, Yezdegard ordered a sackful of earth to be brought and had it loaded on the shoulders of the leader, saying, "This is all the tribute that you will get from me. Inform your general that Rustam (the Persian general) will shortly bury the entire Arab army at Kudesia." But the leader, a man called Asim Amin, willingly bore the burden and departed. When Rustam, the Persian general (no relation of the legendary Paladin) returned, he sensed the symbolic import of having handed over the earth of Persia to the Arab. He sent men in pursuit, but the Muslims had crossed the borders. Amin appeared before his general and flung the sack of earth triumphantly in front of him, shouting, "The Persian soil is ours!"

'But at the battle of Kudesia it was not the Arabs who were buried, but the Persian corpses which were left to the birds after many days of fighting, the issue of the battle having been decided eventually by the veering of the wind, the dust blinding the Persian hosts.

'Yezdegard regrouped his forces, and the battle of Nahavand decided the fate of an empire. The Muslim troops were stirred to their depths by a call from their general, Noman, who said, "Friends! Get ready for conquest or martyrdom! I will sound the *tukbeer* three times. At the first call you will gird your loins, at the second mount your horses and at the third point your spears towards the enemy and rush towards victory or paradise! As for me," said Noman ecstatically, "I will die a martyr." And he did die on the field, but the Arabs won the battle. After that a hundred thousand people were converted every day. Do you realize, my daughter? With a sword in one hand and the Holy Book in the other the Arab hosts went around the country offering death or conversion.'

No homily was necessary, thought Ardeshir. If she still did not get the message, the less said the better. He got up fatigued, his entire strength drained out of him. Even as he pushed back his chair it struck him, inexplicably, that old age had come upon him at the moment. He could feel it that instant, both in his psyche and in his bones, as if through a flash of apprehension. Yes, he realized, the earlier he was prepared for old age, black and brittle as charcoal, the better for him. Yet such is the duplicity of human nature that even as he moved off Ardeshir found himself rummaging in the dregs of satisfaction. He hadn't railed against anybody, hadn't embittered his mouth by the use of wanton expletives, had not succumbed to the exhilaration of hatred. He had placed the facts before Arnavaz as he had found them, and perhaps in the process, opened up a new vista for her. And that was that. He could do no more.

Half an hour later Arnavaz left the house, hailed a cab, got down at Grindlay's Bank and walked into Anwar's office, taking care to bolt the door behind her. She told him clearly that if they were to get married it had to be today. It was not as if they had not discussed matrimony earlier.

'Calm yourself,' said Anwar. 'Relax. Let me get you a cold drink and a sandwich. But for God's sake calm yourself!'

But she was adamant. 'I'm perfectly normal! I am absolutely calm! What is more, I am fully in possession of my faculties! But we either get married today or never!'

There was an argument. 'I told you I have to soften up my parents! After all, they are not going to take kindly to this! But you think only of yourself. Why can't we wait for a few more days? Why the damned hurry?'

'Today or never,' she said, and he noticed her eyes turning into hard bits of quartz. He gave up. After that it was a frenzied scramble, phoning up a few friends, rushing to a mosque in Old Delhi and making a bushy-bearded maulvi agree to act as the Qazi and perform the ceremony, booking a deluxe suite in a hotel—he did not want to face an enraged father-in-law at his door—and booking a flight for Srinagar the next day. In between numerous telephone calls he asked her, 'I hope you've brought a sari! Surely you don't mean to get married in this?' He pointed almost accusingly at the midi she was wearing. Arnavaz assured him that she had taken care to put half a dozen saris in her bag. They moved to the hotel where the Qazi had agreed to perform the nikah. As he was getting down from the car, he asked her rather casually, 'I hope you've thought of a name.'

'Name?'

'Just symbolic, darling, but you will need another "name" after marriage, a Muslim name. Surely you understand that?'

Suddenly her eyes filled and she had to make an effort to hold back her tears. 'But what's wrong with Arnavaz? It's a Persian name.'

'Nothing's wrong with Arnavaz. It's a lovely name and you will always be Arnavaz to me, darling. But the Qazi will want another name immediately after the conversion ceremony. What do you think of Ayesha?'

She somehow felt that he had thought of the name earlier, that it had not occurred to him at the spur of the moment.

The ceremonies were over in a trice. The hollow-cheeked Qazi was brisk. He read the Fatihah (the first chapter of the Koran) and the durud, or blessing, and ran through the Kalimah, or creed

('There is no Deity but God, and Muhammad is the Prophet of God'). Then he raised his hands and intoned, 'O great God! Grant that mutual love may reign between this couple, as it existed between Adam and Eve, Abraham and Sarah, Joseph and Zulekha, Moses and Zipporah, Muhammad and Ayesha, Ali and Fatimah.' Anwar's friends embraced him. She had not had the presence of mind to have asked any of her friends to be present.

At eight in the evening she phoned up her mother and with a catch in her voice told her all that had happened as briefly, and hence as mercifully, as possible. 'Don't wait for me, Mummy,' she said, and put down the phone. Numbed as she was, Firoza noticed the catch in the throat, as if a deep draught of air had suddenly been sucked in, though the voice, as always, had come over clear and deep.

There were sudden confabulations with a handful of friends, a call or two to Bombay to convey the devastating news, and they decided to wait. Just burrow in and wait for better sense to dawn on the couple so that they would return early from Srinagar to enable the parents to at least hold a formal reception. That would surely be more graceful than an elopement.

For two days Ardeshir sat indoors. The noise of the traffic streaming past the Old Fort filtered into his mind, an insidious patchwork of sound that at times blotted out everything else. On the third day the desire for company and for a long walk became overwhelming. He had felt claustrophobic. His mind was fit to burst with those long streamers of thought all falling into place, like the coils of some mythical, endless serpent settling in for the night. He did not notice the pigeons roosting on the domes of the Old Fort. But he could not help noting the candles being lit at the graves with which the sidewalk was studded. The word Traducean somehow kept elbowing into his mind, but the meaning eluded him. He recalled having read an article on Traduceans but could not recollect a thing at the moment.

'A dying race,' he said to himself aloud, 'a dying race. If only she had paid heed to the fact that Parsees were declining at the rate of a thousand a year. At this rate of statistical decline one could give them another eighty-five years. And then they could join the ancient Romans and the Egyptians and find a nook for themselves in the mummy-wraps of history.' He started talking to himself aloud. His thoughts, his passions, were too strong to be quarantined in the mind any longer. He found himself unequal to wrestle with them and dam the flow and feeling of his now desperate interior world.

His attention was drawn to the triple-domed mosque nestling in a plant nursery. He recalled that the signboard here once read 'All Kind Plants Sold Here', till some spoilsport had corrected it and inserted 'of' between the words 'Kind' and 'Plants'. He saw a variety of flame-tipped crotons in flowerpots covering the entire range from rust to russet. Adjacent to the mosque, on the sidewalk, a taxi stand had come up around the grave of a Muslim saint. A few burly Sardars were sitting on folding chairs, playing cards. But they took care to keep the grave covered with marigolds. One of them was lighting a candle in a crypt carved out in the headstone of the grave. A momentary peace descended on him at the sight of the candles being lit. He walked back as dusk set in, his meditation darkening to melancholy.

On his return he looked up the dictionary for 'Traducean' and found it meant one who believes that children receive the soul as well as the body from their parents through natural generation. Well, she certainly did not receive my soul, he said to himself emphatically. The earlier I forget about the Traduceans the better. I am damned if I'm going to add guilt to my existing woes, he thought.

His domestic, Shyam Singh, came in to bolt the windows and secure the fastenings. And suddenly it occurred to Ardeshir that all this was hardly any use. Whatever evil had to enter his house had already got in. He corrected himself. It was innocence which had flown out. But didn't that mean the same thing, the entry of evil and the exit of innocence?

'Shyam Singh,' he said, 'let us get some fresh air. Leave the windows as they are. The same goes for the fastenings. Go and relax. Who's going to waste a night trying to rob an old couple?'

Shyam Singh laughed a little uncertainly, not knowing how to respond.

'Go home, go home,' said Ardeshir, 'the world cannot rob me of anything further now! It has done its damnedest already.' What did an unlatched door or a window left open matter when a new vista was opening up in front of him, melancholic and bitter, to be sure, but a vista nonetheless, a gateway to the vast history of human loss, stretching back perhaps to Eden? Relaxing on his armchair in the verandah he found the frail silhouette of Arnavaz adrift on his memories. And a yearning for his daughter gripped him, for her translucent, porcelain-smooth face and her voice, deep-throated as a cello.

The Long Night of the Bhikshu

The evening had moved in on him almost unsuspectingly, grey cloud leading to grey drizzle. It was when the bullfrogs started croaking that he realized it was dark. They were never really vocal while it was light. The pond was a remnant of what was once a jheel, a sort of watering hole for wild elephants. Those days were long past. The jheel had now shrivelled with age, drying slowly at the edges, each sliver of caked mud being grabbed by frantic peasants as they went about adding to their holdings. The village would soon be arriving at the pond, he thought.

He had always known that a day *would* come

when his window would open out on nothing. Simply nothing. It bothered him. Nothingness was perhaps something you could put into a void. You couldn't. The void would not be a void if you could place something in it. And one had to distinguish nothingness from somethingness. If nothing was nothing, you really couldn't get hold of it and plonk it someplace—certainly not in a non-existent bowl which went by the name 'void'. He was clutching at the straws of his logic and wouldn't let go.

The Bhikshu started mumbling. It didn't strike him that his speech was a bit slurred and his listener was not attentive. You could not accuse him of lip-reading, for the fellow he was speaking to had his back to the Bhikshu. And the Bhikshu was on one of his trips to the past. In his younger days, he was saying, he had wondered about things like whether existence had a hold, however tenuous, on permanence. After all, you lived, you ate, drank, loved, died. All this could not be maya or mithya. He had left all that behind. All he wanted was tranquillity, the night around him, the chirr of the cicada and the croak of the bullfrog.

For some months now he had grown used to talking to the scarecrow. The guava orchard was an adjunct to his hut and the scarecrow stood there tall and erect and bald, for the raffia had been torn from the coconut shell that passed off for his head. Suppose people overheard? That kind of anxiety flooded his consciousness at times and faded away. It was in the fitness of things that the Bhikshu's scarecrow should be tonsured like a monk.

At first he had been hesitant opening up to the scarecrow. If people heard, they'd think he was mad. Aware that the scarecrow was truly old, older than script perhaps, he wished to speak to him in a dead language. The trouble was he didn't know any dead or dying language, except for a sloka or two and the Gayatri, which in any case he could only mutter to himself, for he was not high enough on the caste ladder to recite it. But that was all in the past tense. He had left those fears behind him as one discards a tattered garment. He had moved on.

He was a latecomer to the Buddha. It was not easy for him to recollect how he came into the fold. It happened. You come upon a stream and drink of its waters. You don't have to explain. You drink because both thirst and water are present at that particular moment. But as he told the scarecrow, even that was not wholly true. Reality is always larger than truth. Yet both fit snugly into each other, truth and reality. He was never sure if the scarecrow had understood.

Every now and then his mind moved into momentary clarity and he would become conscious of the whine and zing of insects, start wondering if he would be there next morning to see the dew glittering on the grass, always presuming there would be dew. A time comes in a man's life when he takes nothing for granted. That moment had arrived for him.

Will and volition had not been his strong suits. His people were not happy. His mother's tongue had clicked like a lizard's. How had doubt leaked into him? she asked. What induced a man to change his gods? There are never any answers to such questions. I haven't changed my gods, Mother, have just moved into a system where there are no gods. How can that be? You can't have a sky without gods—or birds. Don't we all know that Buddha is another avatar of Vishnu? You think your mother is so ignorant, just because she can't sign her name!

He had turned footloose, moving from vihara to vihara, an exile not from his faith so much as from the times, and a family is a part of the times. He moved north towards the mountains. He would work as a farmhand and then get bored with the place and move on. The terraced fields were pale green with rice shoots. The gompas took his breath away, the air clean as crystal, gold-painted roofs, gilded pavilions aflutter with pennants, awhirl with prayer wheels. He fell in love with the autumnal amber of the light here. Everyone was friendly, even the Bhotiya dogs. He worked in the buckwheat fields scattered around the gompa estate. He got to know the shepherds; even their sheep dogs seemed to recognize him and did not growl. And he picked up lore from the scriptures, and knew all the stories of the past lives of the Sakyamuni. Within some years he became a fixture in the landscape.

A time came when the Abbot changed and the

monks started warning him. You will have to give up this, you'll have to give up that. What is life if not full of bonds? But he came to know how the other monks smiled their non-committal smiles, and when cornered, he parted his lips as blandly as they ever did.

He wrote to his mother—it was some years since he had seen her. He wanted to become a bhikshu, he wrote. Alarm bells started ringing in the family. He received letters, never mind if they reached him a month later, asking how he would manage giving up everything. They didn't have a way with words and didn't want to be seen as crude, semi-literate though they were. But he knew what they meant: it was all very well reading the scriptures or closing your eyes and swaying with the prayer wheel. But there was life beyond the pages of a book. He would realize that only when he renounced the world. Renunciation? He had nothing to renounce. If you have nothing, you shed nothing. That's what he wanted to write back, but never did.

Those uneasy dreams of his started two years

or so after monkhood. He began hearing voices, mostly his mother calling someone by name, he didn't know who, saw his house crowded with people, string cots laid out in the guava orchard. He dreamt about a woman walking in her dream, her skin grey as chalky clay, her face sand-smudged, her hair dotted with salt crystals. The burnt-leaf face of his mother flitted through this dream world, her fragile skin turning to flakes, shredded tissue, moth-wings.

When the dreams stopped abruptly he realized Mother was dead. The Abbot of a sudden one day put his hand on the Bhikshu's head and said, 'Son, you've had a trying time,' out of the blue, just like that. That confirmed him in his belief. A year later, calculating from the last time he had dreamt of her, he proceeded to his village, and was not one whit surprised to find he had arrived two days before her barsi, death anniversary. He fed the Brahmins, performed all the rites and within a few days left for the gompa once again.

This time the solitudes troubled him, the scent of the pine, the wind through the cedars. Things were too clean here, rice fields too lush, the river too blue, river-foam too white. This had nothing to do with reality as he had known down below, poverty and squalor, and it struck him hard. That there was life beyond this sojourn in and around the gompa, a temporary assignment in paradise. The monks didn't restrain him as he left for his wanderings in the plains.

From one village to another he would walk, the dust of the Doab, fine and powdery, turning to mud on his sweating shins. He would squat under a shady tree and when the villagers would come to him, showing their palms or even horoscopes, he would send them away. He didn't deal in this kind of hocus-pocus, he would tell them. But he would go to their schools and find the schoolmaster missing, and start talking to the children and teaching them. People would bring him food. A room would be cleared and made available. He would settle disputes, chant his mantra, move his little prayer wheel and tell stories about the Buddha. The hare story always entranced the children, how the hare, no other than the Buddha in his earlier life, had nothing else to give the anchorite, and so had asked him to prepare a fire, and had offered himself as a meal. And one day, as he moved from hamlet to hamlet, he skirted a jheel which he seemed to remember, entered a village that looked familiar and found he was back home.

The house had gone, for the roof had caved in and one didn't know when the mud wall, scribbled over with moss, would disintegrate. He put up a reed hut and a thatch roof over it. The guava orchard was untouched, and the scarecrow. Talking to the scarecrow, he found, was better than talking to someone in his dream. Mr Reed-and-Hessian was not a spectre; he occupied space, boasted of an outline, form.

For a brief moment he was aware that he had been babbling away like that mountain brook near the monastery. He was not sure if the scarecrow heard him at all, for the fellow had not turned round even once. There were moments he thought the scarecrow would seek cover from the drizzle and move in and he half expected to hear the swish and rustle of his coming.

The light has to go out when you are fading, but there was no light here in any case. The drizzle had stopped but the trees still dripped. The wind disappeared somewhere in the silence that seemed to engulf the place now. The owl hooted just once. It was no night for his soliloquies. He slept fitfully, his dreams incoherent and suddenly crowded with faces he half remembered. He thought the moon had come out but all that had flickered in his dream was the round face of a tonsured monk. Even that faded, just as dream and sleep and senses were fading. If the rain could walk out of the sky and leave, what was he doing here on terra firma, which was after all just a sense impression? That is what he had been taught at the gompa. Images came into his mind and frayed away into nothingness. A crow's nest face stood out, and an arm stretched towards him, the palm shaped like a crow's foot. He wanted to call out 'Mother', half expecting her to come and others to follow, including the scarecrow, still as a Buddha in the stillness of the orchard. Somewhere in the shadowy hinterlands of his fading awareness he half expected to hear the swish and the swirl and the lollop of his coming.

Going

Postponement is only another form of neglect. When I put something off I don't just slot it on another diary page. I erase it from the mind. The mind is used to erasures, but nothing is wiped clean for good. Everything has a clock of its own, each anxiety, each problem you choose to face or shove under the rug. A fortnight later you hear the almost subterranean ticking, as the clockhands move across your consciousness. You wake up in the middle of the night to go to the loo and you hear the clock ticking away intermittently. Next morning, as you comb your hair frantically, your lips pursed over a pair of bristling hairpins, the pallu of your sari still not over and across your shoulder—you hear the clock again. This time it is distinctly more audible. Then it starts getting louder by the day and you know you have to grapple with the thing right away, and if you dodge it any further you are liable to rupture a blood vessel, worrying about it.

So I didn't even wait for the weekend, took leave from a frowning principal, and pushed off by bus to my grandmother's place. I was there in less than three hours, and took a cycle rickshaw instead of an auto for the simple reason that the high-pitched crackle of the two-stroke engine, not to mention its fumes, always upset Grandma. There had been no letter from her for a month. Moreover, my mother was holed up in Bombay with a fracture and was also worrying herself to distraction about her mother. I called my grandmother 'Mama' and my mother 'Mummy'. That made things easy. I hadn't seen the old lady since the winter break last year and was prepared for the worst, the face more lined, cup and saucer rattling in her hand as she takes her tea, and the vice-like hold of arthritis over her joints becoming more evident and painful.

She was much frailer than I had anticipated, the bone working its way out of flesh and skin. Time seemed to have burrowed into her cheeks and turned them hollow and her breath wheezed in and out of her tired lungs with some difficulty.

'What have you done to yourself, Mama?'

'We leave ourselves alone. It is age that does things to us, child.'

'Have you been eating enough?'

She just smiled. I knew what she would say. No appetite, bhookh. We'd been over all this before, time and again. I noticed that even a smile cost her some effort, seemed to take an ounce of energy away from her. It was a good half hour later that I got around to asking her why the front door was open.

'Who's going to walk up to open it if someone drops by? You people don't understand. Anyway, the ganga will be back any moment. She's gone to the market.'

Though it was almost sixty years since she came from Matheran and settled in the north, she now and then called her domestics 'gangas'. Her gangas used to change frequently earlier on when she still wore her bristling temper like an armour around her. Now all that had changed and this last domestic, Anjali, had stuck to her these ten years. She lived in an outhouse with her poultry and her goat and her alcoholic husband who earned his living as a gardener of sorts, cutting grass and pottering around the estate. The monsoons were on their way out but they had really given it their best shot this year. And they had taken a toll on the roof tiles. Mama had insisted on a sloping roof and red tiles when this sprawling house was constructed. She wanted to be reminded of home, and home was the Western Ghats, and sheets of blinding rain for four months, chaumasa, and the thunder echoing and re-echoing deafeningly among the hills.

Only now the rains in the north were no longer niggardly as before. The monsoons were the season for birds. When Mama slept off in the afternoon, I came and sat on a cane chair in the verandah and one heard them—the koel, the turtle dove and the large green barbet, its neck expanding and contracting concertina-like as she trilled away. Then a peahen flew in, brown as the pre-monsoon earth, long-legged and delicate, and after surveying the scene with snappy jerks of her head, and coming to the quick conclusion that I didn't matter, she set about pecking away at ant and earthworm. When she decided to leave, she did it in an ungainly manner with a hiss and a susurration, as if the wings could hardly take the weight of her body.

I always had a stronger feeling for Mama than for my mother. I know it is a bit cruel to say it, but then cruel things need to be said. The world can't subsist on kindness alone. I have often had this uncanny feeling that kind words are a veneer behind which hypocrisy hides. Mummy and I never got on. It gives you an eerie feeling when you realize that you have passed more than half your life with a person without ever having met her. Not one long conversation do I remember, when you talk, adult to adult, and bare your soul. And if you are not going to bare your soul, your daughter certainly isn't. Not on your life. First give and then expect something in return. This is barter language,

I know, and I'm feeling queasy using it. I also know that language can only describe an approximation to reality. I often tell my class that language can never tell the whole truth, always presuming that there is a degree of wholeness about truth. The judiciary thinks so, though, and I don't grudge them their smugness and their certitudes. But to return to mother, we never saw eye to eye in regard to most things. Our ages, our respective zamanas, seemed to have passed each other, without much contact. With Mama (that's my grandmother, don't forget) it was different. You reached out to another age and shook hands. You were talking to the past. With mother it was talking to the present just slipping into the past. Where the tenses are in flux, communication becomes dicey.

I was always told that Grandma had a terrible temper. But I never got to see it. It was not just that I was spared her pyrotechnics. She made it a point to be sweet and reasonable even to others in my presence. I resented the fact that my mother wanted to frighten me away from her. It wasn't fair, I thought. Now that I think back, it wasn't fair to mother. It took her some time to realize that you couldn't get a false note out of Mama while I was around. The old lady just refused to let her nerves flare as long as I was with her. How was Mummy to know her mother would be that careful? Children can do that to you, I suppose, bring out this kind of supreme effort from the old.

I still remember my long conversations with her. We were playing chess and I got tired. I couldn't have been more than ten and we got talking and one thing led to another and she started speaking of, well, how I was delivered. Who knows what led us on to this, a hatched egg perhaps in one of her outhouses. We were playing chess on Mama's bed and getting nowhere. We left the board as it was, with the pieces scattered over it like miniature statuary. Mama could go into great detail when she felt like it, and if you're going to tell a child how she came into the world, you better feel like it! Mummy's labour seemed never-ending even after the bag had burst. She was at the end of her tether. Mama and the doctor were asking her to make one more supreme effort, but she just lay down on the table, streaming with sweat. Grandma went out for a few minutes, she couldn't recall why. Perhaps just to get some cool air. It was close to midnight and the month was April, after all, and when she came back I was already there! Was I wailing? 'Of course you were. Everyone cries. Show me one who doesn't!' Did I come out feet first? 'Don't be silly. Everyone comes out head first. You dive into the world!' I have heard that those who come out feet first can cure your backache with a touch of their feet. Dad told me. 'Yes, yes, child, but they are one in a thousand, or ten thousand maybe.' A hundred thousand—I put in my bit. She shrugs her shoulders. A million, I say, a billion, a trillion. She doesn't rebuke me. I quieten down. A little later I ask, do you regret it? 'What?' The fact that you weren't there at the moment when I actually came in? 'You mean came out? Yes, I do regret it,' she says.

It was also Grandma who had warned me against the coming onset of pubescence, pain and blood, the lunar month and the lunar cycle and what have you. Yet when it came, she wasn't there and I started crying and screaming for her. Mother tolerated it for a while and kept asking what was wrong. But by now, I say this through hindsight, I must have been overcome by near hysteria. I was sobbing so much I couldn't breathe. I kept shouting for Grandma and mother kept asking me what was wrong and I wouldn't answer. Then she slapped me—first time she ever did, and that's why it hurt. I am not talking of pain. But it shook me all right and I calmed down, though that may sound like a contradiction. I told her about the pain and the blood and it was suddenly she who looked shaken. She never forgave herself, not for having slapped me, but for not guessing what was wrong with me. After the Baralgan tablet and the hot-water bottle it was she who cried. But I steeled myself and didn't relent for years. Some people are just bad at forgiving.

A pair of large green barbets had got separated, each roosting on a different tree, as they kept calling each other. Their conversation was almost human, not that that's much of a compliment to them, but you could make out that they were talking, each waiting till the other had finished his or her trilling. What exquisite manners! You couldn't see them of course, they merged into the green leaves so perfectly. And as dusk gathered, their calls became more anxious. Then one of them flew to the other and I don't know why I felt that it must have been the male who went to his mate. The females normally have their way in the bird kingdom, or should I say bird queendom? It was time for me to go in as well. Her room suddenly smelt rancid. I found her sheets wet.

'Does this happen often, Mama?' I asked, a bit shaken.

'Does what happen?'

I didn't feel like elaborating. It would humiliate her unnecessarily. I lifted her and plonked her on Grandpa's bed, unused these ten years. She was so light in my arms, I felt frightened, the bones so tender I thought they would break even as I lifted her. The body light as wickerwork, light as a cane chair, the skin so thin that I felt I could see the bones through it. I changed the sheets and her clothes.

'Now you are dry and nice and will feel better. That's a good lady.'

I had started to speak like a nurse. She needed one at that moment. I found her suddenly unwell. Her cheeks appeared a little flushed, her hands warm, her pulse a shade quick. I carefully placed the thermometer under her tongue and found the reading close to 102. I made some tea for her and gave her a Paracetamol tablet to swallow. In less than two hours she started sweating. I changed her sadrah because that muslin vest of hers was drenched with perspiration. I applied some powder on her and gave her another change. She nodded off, her chest heaving regularly, the nose a bit blocked and when she exhaled, the air seemed to whistle through her partially choked nostrils. I switched off the fan, but she appeared uneasy, and I had to switch it on again. I covered her with a chaarsa, a thickly-woven cotton sheet, and fixed her mosquito net. And tucking myself into Grandpa's bed slept a fitful sleep where dreams and anxieties took turn to keep me company.

When I woke up I first took a peep through

the mosquito net. It is always reassuring to observe the regular breathing of the old, the chest heaving up and down, the breath drawn in through a high-pitched whistle. I went out to the verandah with my morning mug of tea hoping to see the peacock this time. If the peahen was around last evening, it could be the male's turn now. You couldn't rule it out, could you? But he wasn't there. The babblers were there instead, half a dozen of them, raucous and frantic as ever, spraying their quick-darting looks in all directions. They should be dying of nervous tension, these birds, I thought. A woodpecker drummed away at the fork of a tree. My face still unwashed, my eye sticky with the leftovers of the night's forgotten dreams, I just sat there with my mug of tea, soaking in the morning and feeling the imperceptible breeze against my skin.

Mama was awake by now and I got a cup of tea ready for her. She wouldn't take it without brushing her teeth first. I put a saucer over her cup so that the tea didn't get cold, helped her by holding a basin at her side as she brushed her teeth. And I sponged her face. I told her about the woodpecker and the half a dozen babblers and was immediately corrected. That was a wu-hoo, not a woodpecker, and the babblers, as always, must have been seven and not six. That was a good sign. When the aged are correcting you it means they feel that they are still in charge. It is when they consent to whatever you say that you need to be wary. Within an hour she felt under the weather and dozed off, after a bowl of milk and sago was spoon-fed to her by Anjali.

It rained and the rain-spouts started gurgling noisily and the babblers sneaked into the verandah waiting for the downpour to end. They were silent for once. Possibly it was the final curtain for the monsoons. With nothing to do I took a close look at Grandma's bookshelves. I pulled out a book on Sanskrit poetry. It had a section on different seasons. A verse by Abhinanda caught my eye:

A cloth of darkness inlaid with fireflies;
flashes of lightning;
the mighty cloud mass
guessed at from the roll of thunder;
a trumpeting of elephants,

an east wind scented by opening buds of ketaki,
and falling rain:
I know not
how a man can bear the nights that can hold
all these
when separated from his love.

There was of course much more of this kind; a verse on the lucky lover who helps his rain-wet love change her dress when she comes to him; another on the cloud that makes the road muddy and washes away the makeup from her face and the red lac from her soles but compensates with the lightning which leads her to her lover. Was it always the woman who went to her lover's house those days? Didn't the men venture out? Or was all adventure the lot of adventuresses, with the men dull and slothful as ever, confined to the wedding couch unless someone infinitely brave strayed, literally, into their bedrooms?

The moment the rains cleared the estate seemed to burst into bird song. We even heard the peafowl, their sharp, short, full-throated cries rising in ascending notes. A flight of parrots screamed into the skies, their wings now flashing, now turning dark as the sun and the cloud cover played hide and seek with each other. The babblers regained their voice and started their furtive pecking once again, and a cool mist rose from the ground, thin and vapoury and yet tangible as silver foil.

Her forehead was burning away once again. This time I called the doctor, a fellow who had been treating her for twenty years. He spent a half hour with her, calling her 'aunty', cracking jokes and even making her laugh. He waived his fees even though I tried hard to force some money on him. 'What is it, Doctor?' I asked.

'It could be virus. Could be old age. How can you tell? You'd need tests and X-rays and things to get to the bottom of it all. And she won't like being moved to clinics. I've prescribed some antibiotics. That should do the trick.'

An hour or so later Mama asked for a bath. I know you are not supposed to give it to people who have fever, but there was a pleading look in her eyes. And why not? Why must you deny even such niggardly pleasures to the old? I gave her a hot bath and thought I'd straight away tuck her into bed and put a blanket over her so that she wouldn't catch a chill. But the old woman was firm about doing her kusti, first winding the sacred thread around her and then opening her prayer book, the *Khordeh Avesta*, and reading from it. I threw a shawl over her. And as soon as she finished and bowed before the portrait of Jarthosth Sahib (Zarathushtra), I made her lie down and slipped a blanket over her. She asked Anjali to get a garland for the Zarathushtra portrait and a toran, a flower-string, to be strung across the door-sill. Anjali's husband, who had not got his fingers around a glass of country liquor as yet, brought the garland and the marigold string. And he swept the drawing room and swabbed the verandah dry. It is uncanny, isn't it, that a half hour's honest work from someone can surprise you at times?

Mama, I have such a sense of calm here I can't express it. I want to write a letter to you, right here, sitting in the verandah, waiting for the peacock who will never come, and watching the clouds drift away. Tranquillity is not a garment one can put on. It has to descend on you on its own. Like rain perhaps, an invisible rain. Or perhaps there is something about the house and you and my days spent here that brings out this sense of peace from the core of my being. Just being here brings it on. Your old shisham doors; the windows which could do with some dusting (after all, how much can Anjali do?); the furniture old and carved and yet not 'antique' in the current chic sense; the lawns not manicured; the gap-toothed roof with some of the tiles missing. (Of course, one can't but not see the patches of damp on the walls, few as they are, where mildew has left its slimy heraldry.) An aroma of age, like the yellowing of language. Things unkempt, yet not gone to seed. I don't know how to express this, Mama, but I am overflowing with feeling. A feeling hard to define. A little love, a little gratitude. Not just for you, but for providence itself, that I am with you at this late moment, that something impelled me to come here at all.

And I feel grateful to the stillness here, which slows one down and seeps into you. Time doesn't tick away here, it ripens, like evening light turning to amber. It slurs past like river water flowing over a pad of moss. I seem to be getting pseudo-lyrical, Mama, and that sure is a danger signal—loss of control. The only thing left now is going overboard with a bit of a splash. (No point in going overboard in silence.)

Suddenly, out of nowhere, the peacock appears, as if he had sprung out of my reverie. It is a bit uncanny—you move out of a rumination and find that the reality in front of you has changed; reality of course meaning flesh and substance and matter. All the rest, things like dream and longing and memory, are vapours from the realm of the spirit. How does that sound, now? Sounds good, doesn't it? It's the closest I have ever got to philosophy. But even according to my scheme of things, the peacock is certainly a part of reality. He is on a trip all his own. He hardly looks down, for he isn't interested in slugs. He wants to show off—the way I was trying to a few lines earlier. His wings scintillate as they slowly fan out. His dance is ungainly but you hardly notice the dance. Your eyes are fixed on the backdrop of his wings. Even as he starts swaying, Anjali comes out to call me. Mama is feeling ill again.

'What is wrong, Mama?' I ask.

'I don't know. *Kai gamtoo nahi.*' I don't feel good. She is rheumy-eyed. I don't know how much of my face her eyes can take in. I notice her wheeze. A whistle seems to go off when she inhales.

'Having trouble with your breathing, Mama?'

She shakes her head. Her hands don't feel warm, nor her brow. She isn't feverish. I phone the doctor all the same. Yes, he'll be there in an hour, he says. She hears me talk to him and cries out, 'Don't call the doctor. He'll only give me another injection. I don't want it.' She extends her arm, asking for the phone.

The whole afternoon she is restless, dozing off fitfully. When she finally wakes up, I notice her sweat-damp hair. Suddenly her eyes, misted as ever, seem to be the only thing alert about her. She seems a little reassured seeing me. The familiar light of my face perhaps sustains her. Holding her fever-warm hands in mine I sit beside her on her bed. A sense of peace and quietude descends on me.

'Can I sit with you like this?' I don't know why I have to ask her. She didn't seem to be taking it amiss, her grand-daughter holding her hands. But now she shakes her head and withdraws her hands. I sit with her for a while but then feel restless. The doctor has still not arrived.

'Can I give you some soup?'

She doesn't answer. But I go into the kitchen all the same and get busy with pots and pans, boiling the vegetables. It will keep my mind away from her. I stand there while the saucepan steams away. Hang on, Grandma, just hang on! Halfway through Anjali comes in and I read fear in her eyes. I switch off the gas and rush to Grandma's room and realize that her face and the expression on the face stand frozen. Her look is kind, compassionate, but iced over all the same. And it is there to stay. For ten minutes I left her and she had to go just then.

ALSO IN TIGERBACKS FROM SPEAKING TIGER

SLICES OF THE MOON SWEPT BY THE WIND

A Novella

Surendranath S.

Translated from the Kannada by Prathibha Nandakumar

> *'I am not like others. I know that. But I do eat like others. And sleep like them. I also cry... But I will not tell you how I look. It's for you to imagine any which way you want to. Whatever your imagination is, I look worse than that.'*

So says the little boy who is writing this story, an intelligent, sensitive mind trapped in a tragically misshapen body. He writes about the world outside, seen from the window of his room: a Muharram procession in which a man with green eyes turns to smile at him; birds that perch on the windowsill like friends; boys who call him 'monkey' and hold out peanuts... And he writes about the world inside: Appa, who harbours a dream that his son will one day go to school, even as he battles his demons at night; Doddakka, his elder sister, who could never get married; Sannakka, his middle sister, who will only accept a suitor who accepts her little brother; Amma, who sells her gold to pay her husband's debts; Hosakka, whom he had given up for dead till she mysteriously reappeared; Anna, his elder brother, who defies his father's wrath to forge a perilous path... Only Tangi, his baby sister, brings some light into the house with her smile. In a dysfunctional universe, it begins to seem that the only 'normal' person is the boy, wise beyond his years.

First published in Kannada, *Slices of the Moon* is an immensely moving glimpse into the mind and heart of a special child.